A MEMOIR OF GRIEF AND WITNESS

WHEN
TO
LET
GO

DANELLE HARMON

OHB

For those who grieved him.
For those whose hearts broke over his death.
For those who could not bear the thought of him drowning.
For those who were angry with me, and never forgave me for
letting him go.

For those who cried for him.
For those who wanted one last sail with him.
For those who wished I had rescued him in the final moments.

And for anyone who has ever loved deeply,
lost painfully,
and carried grief longer than they expected.

This, my dear reader...
This book is for you.

AUTHOR'S NOTE

My first novel was published in 1991...a long time ago now, when I was still a very young woman. But after twenty-one books, all of them historical romances, I found myself unable to write another one.

I was tired. Beaten up quite badly, as so many of us are, by life itself.

What you are about to read is not a romance novel.

I needed to write this book if I am ever to write another.

This is a deeply personal story. Some of you will love it. Some of you will recognize your own lives in it. Some of you may wish I had written something else entirely, and won't finish it. All of that is fair.

What follows is based on a true story. While it takes an unexpected, seemingly impossible form, the events, the grief, and the questions that shape it are all real.

I offer it to you, as it came to me.

Love,
—Danelle

I know, with the certainty of my heart, that life goes on in ways that remain forever mysterious to us all.

— CAPTAIN BRENDAN MERRICK, 1813

1

———

JUNE 25, 2025

The call came in around 11 a.m.

It was the kind you dread—and which remains with you for the rest of your life.

It was my husband, Chris, who had gone over to my mom's house to deliver some medicine for her. I was still in bed—being an insomniac and night owl kind of does that to you—when the phone rang. I picked it up, thinking he was going to tell me he was having trouble filling the prescription.

"You're not going to want to hear this, but I'm here at your mom's house and she's on the floor and—" his voice started to shake "—she's cold, and I think—" his voice was breaking now, laced with panic "—I think she's gone."

I think she's gone.

When his voice reached the word *gone*, the crack that had started with *cold* split fully open, striking that place in the body that reacts before the mind can catch up—like an electric shock. You're stunned. Paralyzed, for a moment. I lay there in the bed. Mom was eighty-six. She lived alone. Moms are supposed to live forever, even if they'd had a fall that ended up in an ER visit thirty-six hours before, and had become housebound, imprisoned by a frail and aging body. I heard Chris telling me that the emergency services were on the way, and a moment later the wail of the sirens through the phone, distant and terrible and growing closer.

In moments like these, we never know how we're going to react. We only remember, long afterward, that we did. I recall hanging up the phone, clinging to hope that maybe he was wrong, that the first responders would get there and they would revive her and that she would be okay, because...moms aren't supposed to die. That moment lasted only a second; in times of paralyzed helplessness, our brains take over on muscle memory. My first thought was my sister. I called her. She lives far away and had to be told. My second call was to the small local pet adoption agency from which I'd found Henry eight weeks before. The little dog needed to be taken out of there and brought to safety.

The aftermath of all this isn't really relevant to the story that I'm about to tell you. Death does what it does, and the wheels of necessity turn after you give the wheel the hard spin. Laurie came immediately and got little Henry, who eventually ended up in a new loving home. The ER services came, pronounced my mother dead on her bedroom floor, and a priest came and gave her last rites (even though she wasn't Catholic, I accepted the offer—her foremothers were, after all, of the faith), and the undertaker came and took her out.

Having set things in motion, I lay back and stared up at the living room ceiling and waited for poor Chris to get home. This space served as my temporary bedroom. My bed had been moved downstairs, and it was where I'd spent pretty much all of the last week and a half.

There was a reason that I wasn't the one to find Mom.

The reason was because my left leg was in an immobilizer, the tibial plateau—whatever that was—fractured after two of our German Shorthaired Pointers, Bradford and Tilley, got into a bloody argument in the kitchen and slammed into my legs, bringing me down. They had gotten into a fight because their mother, Maisie, was dying of bladder cancer, and I was cooking chicken for her—good enough, apparently, to be worth bickering over. Down I went, at 11 p.m., the kitchen perfumed with chicken breast and dog blood and my own fear as I lay there unable to get up, knowing that this was bad.

Really bad.

And it was. Like, total immobility and being non-weight-bearing bad for six weeks, stuck in bed with only crutches, a walker, and a wheelchair.

I couldn't get outside.

I couldn't even take care of my elderly mother.

A fellow author friend once told me I'm resilient. I was in my thirties then, not my early sixties as I am now, and looking back, I had no idea what "resilient" really meant because I hadn't been as tested then, as life would test me in the years to follow.

As 2025 would almost break me.

In a year that would start with our Westminster Select Bitch, Maisie, being diagnosed with transitional cell carcinoma, leading to thousands of dollars' worth of chemo that bought her no time, only suffering, it was—as Queen Elizabeth II once described her own awful year—my "annus horribilis," a year in which I lost our sweet Maisie, my mobility and independence, and my mother all within two weeks of each other.

It started with bad news, and moved straight into loss upon loss upon loss.

It ended with a miracle.

2

———

JULY, 2025

It's a blistering hot day. I lie in bed—I mean, where else would I go? What is there to do? I'm trapped here in the house, an old farmhouse, not set up for a person in my disabled state.

I can't get outside without help. The crutches and hopping on one leg, plus the sloping concrete to get out of the house and onto the driveway, are dangerous. They tip me forward and scare me. The stone steps that lead out onto the back patio are non-negotiable now. It's a struggle to even get to the refrigerator and get the door open.

I turn onto my side and stare out the window, past the smears of dog-nose ectoplasm, into a day outside that excludes me.

The trees across the street are waving in a gentle breeze, and my soul aches to be free of this house and out into the day. I touch the window. I should probably clean it, but that dog snot is partially Maisie's, and I just can't. As she got sicker, she'd insist on sliding beneath the covers and curling herself up against the curve of my body. She must've known she was dying. I was her safe haven.

The nights are hard now. With nothing to do all day— all the musculature and endurance I'd built from lap-swim-

5

ming are melting into sludge—my aging body aches for exercise it cannot get. I can't make it tired enough to sleep when all I can do all day is lie around in bed, or the recliner, and wait for the next orthopedic appointment. The next X-ray to see how much healing may or may not have ensued.

And the worries...will the leg ever be the same again? Will I be able to go to the Oasis concert down in New Jersey that I've waited all these years to see? How much more will this horrible year take from me?

I turn over again. I can't get comfortable in this stupid brace, and though I'm allowed to take it off in bed, my broken leg craves the support and stability it offers; not only is the bone damaged, but what's left of my meniscus also got badly torn when the two idiots slammed into me. Turning over makes the meniscus unhappy; to do so, I must stiffen the leg, hold the thing in my hands at the knee joint, steady it so the cartilage doesn't get twisted, and ease onto my side.

There comes a time when rest is boring.

Because it's all you can do.

While I lie there replaying the injury—what I should've done to prevent it—I realize, for the second time in two years, that my body is no longer the reliably strong thing it used to be. I'd broken a bone (and suffered a severe ankle sprain) in 2023 as well, when our oldest German Shorthaired Pointer, Brendan, yanked me off my feet and down a small ravine as he'd gone after something, probably a rabbit, off in the darkness. Age and its pals—osteoporosis, arthritis, chronic back pain—are relentlessly stealing the things I took for granted. The things I love.

The things that have defined me.

Except for my writing. It hasn't yet taken that, I think, as I lie there on the bed staring up at the ceiling that has become far too familiar to me.

But I can't write.

Six weeks confined and off my feet should've been the perfect recipe for making lemonade out of this giant lemon, to use this forced immobility to write my next novel. After all, the book has been waiting for years for me to get my act together. I owe my readers a happy conclusion for Lord Brookhampton, otherwise known as Perry, last seen suffering the effects of PTSD and sinking further and further into darkness.

Perry needed rescuing. My readers want him to be okay.

I have no writerly mojo to deal with Perry.

I can't even deal with myself.

The day is closing in. Outside, late evening sun slants across the grass and shrubbery beyond my window. It hits the dog smears on the century-old window glass, and I feel a pang for Maisie, then guilt, because she was a dog, and I should be grieving my mother—and I do.

I have nowhere to put the grief. Nowhere to put my body that is sick of resting.

So I turn over once more, trying to get comfortable, the steady hum of the air conditioner and the deep, measured breathing of my dog Brendan, the only sounds in the room. Chris is out doing all the chores I cannot do...taking care of our horse, the chickens, the yard, the meals. I stare across the room into nothingness. The world, for me, has stopped. I feel a tear soaking the pillow beneath my eye. Brendan stretches, his aging body pressing against my own; his dark chocolate eyes crack open to check on me for a moment, and he falls back asleep. I'm sick of being in this bed, but he doesn't mind having me all to himself, not having to share me with the two idiots who put me here, and he'll stay here all day, if I want.

And he's done just that.

I feel the raw, empty spot in the bed where Maisie should be sleeping, and the tears begin to burn. I think of my mom's purple coffin sitting there in the hot summer sun of the cemetery a few days ago, a week, whatever it was, a small gathering of family and friends, and me in a wheelchair.

I curse my fragile bones, and somewhere between my last memory of the wetness beneath my pillowed cheek, I feel myself drifting. Sleep, at last.

Because what else is there to do?

3

I am no longer alone.

I can sense it in my bones. Maybe it's Maisie, come to visit me in a dream...or my mother. Maybe they'll be together, Mom holding Maisie's leash, both of them whole, healthy—and young again. People who lose loved ones fill YouTube and TikTok with stories of visitations, of their loved ones coming to visit in apparitions, dreams, even the tap of a bird on an outside window. I've never had that sort of experience. I don't see ghosts, have premonitions, or experiences I can't explain. Mom was a bit on the psychic side; I am not. I feel curiously unmoored, and as I turn over in bed, knowing I'm not alone, I expect—*hope*—to see Mom.

Maisie.

Instead, a man is standing there.

"Hello," he says, warmly.

He's about thirty, maybe a little older. It's hard to tell, because he's got a young face, but there's a touch of weathering along the corners of his eyes, either from humor, squinting against the sun, or both. His eyes themselves, a warm caramel-amber, are not quite gold, nor quite brown, and not quite russet, but a warm hot toddy of all three.

The eyes.

"I know you," I say simply. The words come out of my mouth in a whisper, my voice still trapped in my larynx. "I... *know* you."

He just looks at me in understanding, a little smile beginning to tug at his mouth at my stupefaction from what I'm looking at. He knows I'm a wordsmith. And he seems to find it just a little bit amusing that his presence has struck me dumb.

"Yes, you do," he answers, and his smile spreads then, affirming that the little crinkle lines on the outside of his eyes were indeed put there by the innate good humor and optimism that I know he has.

I know because I was the one who put them there.

But I'll get to that shortly. For now, I just want to tell you about what happened, because while it made no sense in the moment, it most certainly did later.

Much later.

Back to that moment...it dawns on me, then, that he's standing here in his work uniform. I'm not talking about the traditional clothing we think of when we consider "uniform"—it's not a pilot's dark coat with the little bars on the shoulders, it's not a doctor's or my local vet's scrubs, it's not even something like the town cops or local EMTs wear when one thinks of the word.

It's a blue woolen coat, a bit worn, fitting his long, lean, lanky frame with familiarity, the red lapels and turned-back cuffs echoing the red tones in his deep chestnut hair and a row of buttons trailing down the front. There are salt stains on it; I know it's salt because I can smell it. Not table salt, but ocean salt. Sea salt. Brine. He doesn't look like 2025. He doesn't smell sterilized, but like a mix of the sea, wool, whatever soap he uses. Earthy. Natural. I can see his linen shirt beneath, hand-sewn with someone's love, each stitch faintly imperfect, irregular, the real thing and not what the local reenactors down in Lexington and Concord wear, but a shirt and a coat that aren't pretending to be anything but what they are.

A working uniform.

"You look a bit shocked to see me," he says, and there, in his warm, kind eyes, a slight cajoling. He tilts his head just a bit to the side, and I can see that he's enjoying this.

Whatever "this" is, because I certainly don't know.

"I know you're confused," he murmurs, taking off the coat. He looks around this living-room-turned-bedroom, trying to find a place to put it, and settles it on the arm of the sofa. "I see that New England summers are just as hot as they ever were. You don't mind, do you?"

"M-mind?" I still can't find my voice.

"Wool in July...not a good mix," he says, his eyes twinkling with mischief, and I agree, and just stare at him.

He is all that I imagined—literally—that he would be. And more. And there are little details I didn't catch when I saw him in my imagination and invited him into the pages of my second novel, published all those years ago in 1992. I was a young writer then, still feeling my way, inexperienced and naïve and learning my craft. Nineteen more books would follow—a few of which he would reappear in. Yes, there was the thick, slightly curling chestnut hair, the set of his eyebrows, the shape of his nose, his smiling mouth, the angle of his jaw. But even the best imagination (and mine is pretty darned good) cannot quite capture or prepare you for the real thing. No book cover I'd ever picked out had quite caught him. Even my imagination had painted something nebulous, just out of reach.

This man is not out of reach.

He's standing right in front of me and he's thoroughly three-dimensional.

His grin is infectious. It's spreading, and I see now that he's carrying his tricorn under his arm, just like a proper gentleman would. He places it neatly down on the coat, and runs a hand through his hair, which the tricorn must've flattened before he arrived here in this living room that now serves as my bedroom. The grin—its very essence is a vaccine into my hurting soul, and I feel myself smiling in return.

"No...it is not a good mix," I say, playing along with this strange madness. "It's T-shirt and shorts weather. Not...long sleeved linen shirts, wool coats, and...breeches."

His brow furrows a bit, and I realize he has no idea what a T-shirt and shorts are.

Of course he wouldn't.

This is nuts, I think.

His smile is suddenly not quite so certain. It feels like the day does when a cloud is skirting the sun, the bright warmth still there, but shadowed. "Are you not happy to see me, Danelle?"

Geez, that accent. It's even more mellifluous and soothing in person than it was in my head when I first heard it. It's musical, lyrical, voice as music itself—Irish. Or Irish, softened by the many years he spent in the officer ranks of the Royal Navy. Sometimes, when I can't sleep (which is most of them), I open an app on my phone that lets me listen to Air Traffic Control out of Shannon Airport in Ireland. There's a particular guy there directing high-altitude planes in from over the North Atlantic late, late at night, and his voice is smooth, reassuring, musical.

Brendan's voice is like this.

And yes, it *is* Brendan. Like the Saint. Like my dog.

Brendan.

THAT Brendan.

I feel myself flushing red, my skin hot despite the air conditioning, because now I'm embarrassed. "If I expected anyone in a dream, it was Maisie. Or my Mom," I offer lamely, although seeing *him* is something I never expected in a million years. That's a realm reserved for prophecy, remembrances, fears, and dead loved ones.

This man is none of that. And he's looking at my leg. The left one, strapped into the immobilizer, the Velcro straps curling, the black ugliness of the thing already wearing the uniform of *my* house—dog hair. White, short ones. Some of them, Maisie's. I feel tears starting to well.

"I see that you're marooned...not able to enjoy this fine day," he says softly, and now the laughter really *is* gone from his eyes, and in its place, a deep, soul-acknowledging compassion that touches something in my heart and makes it clench its fist around my emotions, and squeezes the tears, already poised there, up from my sinuses. They flood my eyes and I look away. The room is blurry through them, like looking underwater.

I can't speak.

"I understand, now," he says, and stretches out a hand. "Come, get up. I want to see my town—Newburyport. I want to see how it's changed, and I want you to be the one to show me."

Of all the times to be laid up. A chance to actually inhabit space with my most beloved creation and I can't even freaking walk. "I can't," I say, and this time, the tears are rolling down my cheeks and I know I'm not only injured physically, emotionally, and spiritually—yes, spiritually, because I've been in a dark night of the soul for the past fifteen years—but in a place of endurance. This summer has taken so much...I'm depleted.

At the end of my reserves.

His fingers are still outstretched. His hand looks exactly as it did when I wrote about him all those years ago—masculine but elegant, the fingers long, the same ones I'd seen holding a sketchbook while musket balls flew past his head and shot slapped through the mainsail arcing out beyond his shoulder and Liam, poor Liam, stood there yelling for him to get his head out of the clouds and get to work on being a privateer captain before they all got blown to kingdom come. How he'd liked to tease poor Liam, winding him up more and more, until, on the verge of Liam bug-eyed and completely losing it, he'd laugh, toss the sketchpad aside, and get to work with cutting precision, giving some order that would instantly display the clever, Royal Navy-trained mind behind those warm amber eyes—and save the day.

Every time.

"Go ahead," he says, and the little grin is coming back, playing around with the corner of his mouth. "Take my hand. I'm not ethereal, you know. I'm not a spirit, or a ghost. I'm really here. And don't worry about your broken leg. It won't trouble you."

"But—"

He just smiles and pulls me to my feet. "Let's go," he says. "I'm eager to see Newburyport." And as I stand on my suddenly sound leg and find it moving beneath me as it always had, carrying weight that's not supposed to be on it for several more weeks, I rip the Velcroed straps apart and discard the thing, wrap my fingers tightly around his, and leave the bed.

I can't wait to show him his town.

My town.

Our town.

4

———

Chris and I, with our toddler daughter, our cat, and two German Shorthaired Pointers, sold our antique home in Newburyport in 2001, closing on the same day the Twin Towers were annihilated by jets turned into bombs and the world as we'd known it changed forever.

I still remember standing in our kitchen with the city's fire chief as he was inspecting our smoke alarms while the TV in the background blared in real time, and the chief's quiet comment that all those men, weighed down by their gear as they trudged skywards—toward a heaven they would soon reach quite literally—were likely lost.

It was our dream house. Chris and I had looked at dozens of homes when we moved back here from England, but this house...this was the one. It was ours. Built sometime between 1799 and 1806, it was rooted in my favorite era, in my favorite little city. It was within smell and sight of the Merrimack River's mouth, and the open Atlantic.

But my father had died earlier in the year, leaving my sister and me our childhood home several miles inland. My sister didn't want it—neither did I, really—but I couldn't let the memories, my place of refuge from childhood bullies and later mere adulting, go to strangers. I'm sentimental like that.

Too much so.

That childhood house we moved into, built in 1900, was too new for my eighteenth-century heart. It sits near the same Merrimack that winds its way down from New Hampshire to the Atlantic some nine miles away, but it is not Newburyport. What it did, and continues to offer, is space: two acres on a quiet dead-end street, room for a child, for animals, for a life that needed more breathing room. And so, with heartache, we sold our dream home, bought out my sister's half of the family house, and moved in.

It isn't relevant here how hard those early years were, walking through grief inside my father's house. What matters is this: I missed Newburyport—and I always would. But the city changed. It grew crowded and expensive and performative in ways that made it feel less like home, less like the working seaport I loved, and more like a place curated for visitors rather than those who had lived their lives there. There was no going back.

Maybe Chris and I were wise to leave when we did.

But those days feel far away now.

Occasionally, something in Newburyport still stops me short—something that looks as though it belongs. And I'm reminded of the day I was working in nearby Amesbury back in the mid-1980s and decided, on my lunchbreak, to go see the reproduction tall ship visiting Newburyport, and get a tour of her deck.

As I followed the river into the city, and the old, restored brick buildings of Market Square came into view—there, beyond the buildings, beyond the shade trees of the parking lot bordering the Merrimack—I saw her masts. They towered over everything: the trees, the city, reality itself, strangely belonging, strangely out of place, a whisper of the historic amongst the modernity. And it wasn't just their height; it was their slant, the way they angled aft, giving her a look of predatory beauty. She was a queen, that ship, on a tour made royal by her very presence, and I fell in love with her, and eighteenth-century ships, in that moment.

That ship would go on to inspire a living, breathing character who, in 1813, would carry her designer and captain to his own death.

Her name was *Pride of Baltimore*.

Her namesake was *Kestrel*.

And the captain of said *Kestrel* is the man in whose hand I now find my own.

5

———

I'm thinking of all of this—flashes of it, really—as Brendan asks to see the city he left in 1813 for the trip to Barbados, never to return—unless whatever this experience I'm having now, counts. And of course it doesn't, because it's not real.

(Is it?)

He was an older man then, mid-sixties. The one walking beside me is half that age, looking up at the buildings, remarking that when he was last here, most were built of wood, before the 1811 fire wiped them all out. He tells me that brick seems to have held up well.

He is pointing out the things that must be strange to him, but I want him to experience some of it for himself. We head into one of the boutique clothing and gift shops on Pleasant Street. As the door opens, the young woman behind the counter glances up with idle boredom at the sound of the bell, reflexively back down at her phone and then immediately her head jerks back up—she's staring at Brendan, and so, I see, are some of the customers—and not just the younger ones.

It's not because of the fact he's still wearing his curling chestnut hair in the queue, or that his shirt looks a bit old fashioned. It's *him*. He's running his fingers over the T-shirts folded neatly on a shelf, musing about sizes—what are small, medium, large?—completely oblivious to the attention.

He's tall, lean, a good six feet, maybe an inch or two more—I smile as I remember the scene in *Captain Of My Heart* where his feet were hanging over the footrail of the bed because of that height. It's the moment after which Matthew Ashton rescues him from a night in the sea, when Brendan—still recovering—first meets Matthew's sister Mira, the feisty little hoyden who unsettled him, intrigued him—and captured his heart.

Does Mira know he's here? I think oddly.

He selects one of the shirts; it's got "NEWBURYPORT" written across it, and he grins with delight, as though he's just discovered a plane ticket to Disney World.

"I'll try this one on," he says, and heads to the dressing room.

Female eyes are following him. One woman had been about to leave the shop; she pretends an excuse to stay, fingering some scarves, her eyes watching the dressing room in the mirror for his emergence. They've not only seen his disarmingly handsome face, and been caught up in his easy charisma. Now his warm, musical Connemaran accent—polished by the precision of Royal Navy English—has sealed things.

Nobody's going anywhere.

He emerges a few moments later, quite amused, a little self-conscious in the most endearing way as he finds the mirror and gazes at his reflection. The shirt is grey; its soft cotton kisses the muscles beneath, emphasizes the breadth of his shoulders, his strong wiry arms, the way his waist narrows down into khaki trousers he's somehow acquired. The women have gone still. Two of them are leaning in close, whispering behind their hands.

He's utterly oblivious to the quiet damage he's doing.

"Strange, how people wear letters on their clothing... rather like a ship's transom. An identification, of some sort. Anyhow...it's lovely in grey," he says. "But I quite like the blue one as well."

I just smile, letting him make his decision. He thinks about it for a moment.

"I'll take the blue," he says happily. "It'll make a nice souvenir to bring home with me."

He returns to the dressing room and emerges wearing his choice. Their eyes follow us after it's paid for and we're leaving the shop.

Back out on Pleasant Street we go. The scent of pizza is in the air, as well as the nearby ocean; the tide must be coming in, he remarks casually. He doesn't seem surprised or shocked by anything, as if he's accepted all of this because he'd never really left it. Maybe he just wanted to experience it with me.

Either way, his attention seems to be more on me, now, than on his surroundings—as though he's here not for a tour of the city, not to have me show him something, but because he wants to show *me* something.

I notice this when, in response to his questions, I'm talking about Mom. About Maisie. About how much has narrowed.

How I can no longer enjoy the things that defined me—not in some abstract way, but physically. I can't run a dog around a show ring anymore. I can't stand for more than five minutes without my back screaming. I can't ride my horse. A childhood eyesight issue has returned.

It's not one loss. It's the accumulation.

All the small permissions that once made up a self, quietly revoked.

I no longer trust the author of my life, the way Brendan seems to trust the author of his.

Me.

And he must have trusted his author because I sure did put him through a lot.

Including death.

But I never abandoned him to randomness, cruelty for the sake of spectacle, or existence without a clear path forward. His life had meaning. It had poetry. Even his death —which affected me so badly it put me in the emergency room of the Anna Jaques Hospital with a panic attack when I wrote it—had meaning, his end honoring who he was. Had he been the author of his own book I suspect he'd have written it exactly the same way.

He trusted me, implicitly.

And here I am, in the endlessly long dark night of my spiritual soul, losing more and more light with this summer of loss, unable to trust my creator. My author. The randomness that has become my life, the losses of everything I am and ever was, the thought that everything might be meaningless, that at the end you just die, anyhow.

I've lost trust.

And if I'm not careful, I'm going to lose faith.

Maybe I already have.

I don't notice when we stop walking.

He's looking at me, seeing things I can't understand, and he's saying something about trust, as if he can read my mind. As if he can absorb my pain, and the betrayal I feel over what life was supposed to look like, into the deepest recesses of his own heart.

And now we're outside a narrow door in some street in Newburyport, this one still uneven with old cobbles, and the door has no sign, no glass, just a plain handle worn smooth by hands that trusted it would open.

"I don't remember that being here," I say.

"You wouldn't," he replies.

He rubs his jaw.

I'm thinking of him now—caring about him, because I always did—and asking him if he can still feel pain.

"I feel everything I did in my living years," he says, and pushing open the door, he leads me inside a building.

And here, things get even stranger, because it's a dentist's office; more precisely, an oral surgeon's, and we're standing in a room that is quiet and bright in that neutral, unthreatening way meant to calm people who are frightened. Why doesn't he need an appointment? How are there already X-rays saying he's got impacted wisdom teeth, and it's all set up for him, just like that? Someone's handing him a clipboard. He's filling out the consent forms.

I glimpse a chair in an adjoining room that manages to look neither threatening nor comforting, simply awaiting its purpose, and fear wraps a cold fist around the base of my spine.

I want to leave.

Now.

But someone's giving him a pen, and he takes it without hesitation and begins to sign, flipping pages with the ease of a man who is confident and at ease with a big decision. A man who's already decided that staying present matters more than knowing every outcome.

"Aren't you even going to look at what you're signing?" I ask, incredulous.

"That's of no matter," he replies mildly. "The choice has already been made."

I take the moment to look at his penmanship; I never did get to see that with my previous authorly encounters with him, and I note how he writes like any man of his time would—elegant flourishes, sweeping curves—when writing was still more than communication; it was art, it was commitment, it was the visible acceptance of conse-quence. I notice his moment of amused surprise that this pen in his hand doesn't have a quill tip, or an ink pot feeding its constant need for more ink, and the quiet delight he takes in sending the instrument across the signature lines without the pen ever having to catch its breath.

He's signing forms for something unknown and potentially dangerous (and I know this because I know that this man cannot even drink alcohol without it making him sick —and he's consenting to anesthesia? What?), and he's more interested in the pen?

I can't help it; I stare at him, my face frozen in incredulity. Fascination. Because while I might have authored him, he's very much his own person, and there's a heck of a lot that I still don't know about him.

The person at the counter looks at me, then at him. "She can stay?"

"She will," he answers, before I can.

No argument. No explanation. Just authorship acknowledged.

I want to bolt.

My leg, still strangely intact, says I can.

I will never leave you, he'd vowed to his beloved Mira.

But I had left him.

I won't leave him now.

The chair waits.

He sits down. Not stiffly. Not bravely. He simply sits, settles, as though this is no different from lowering himself into a cabin bunk after a long watch.

His manner is resolved, just as it was when he laid his tricorn on *Kestrel*'s binnacle, saluted the deck, and went below knowing his choice was made.

To step into what he had already accepted.

My heart is racing, and my skin is suddenly cold, and I want to save him from this strange experience as I've wished for the past dozen years that I could've saved him from the sinking ship and what I believed awaited him.

"You don't have to do this," I plead. "You don't have to relinquish control. You can wait. You don't even know who these people are."

He shrugs, and the little smile is there in his eyes, confident. Himself.

"I know how it ends."

Not bravado. Not prophecy.

Acceptance.

I'm headed for another ER visit at this rate, but he's resolute. He swings his long legs up and onto the lower half of the chair. I see the Newburyport T-shirt stretch across his pectorals, see it hollow down into his abdomen on the exhale as he settles himself.

They tilt the chair back. He doesn't grip the arms but just crosses his own over that same chest.

He's relaxed.

Trusting.

He turns his head slightly so he can see me, and reaches out a hand. Puts it in mine.

"Don't look so terrified," he says, teasing me. "You'd think I was going to sea for the first time!"

"This is not funny," I manage, thinking of his sensitivity to things that shouldn't be in the body, like alcohol.

"No," he agrees, his eyes warming even more, now crinkling a bit at the corners. And then he's serious once more. "But it's necessary."

They bring the mask closer. He watches it approach with mild curiosity, then looks back at me.

"This is the part," he says quietly, "where we let go of staying awake. Of staying vigilant. Of fiercely guarding control. It's the part when learning what trust in the author actually means. The part where trust stops being an idea and becomes an action." His gaze holds mine, and with a pointed intention, he adds, "The part where we learn when to let go."

I stare at him.

What trust in the author actually means.

I want to haul him out of there. "I'm not the one in the chair."

"No, you're the one who needs to see it," he says gently, as if this has always been the point.

The mask settles over his face. He keeps his eyes on mine —steady, untroubled—until the very last moment.

Then, just before the medicine takes him, he says, almost conversationally, "I'll be back before you've finished worrying."

His eyes slide sideways, begin to close. His head follows.

And he's gone.

Just like that. No drama. No struggle. No fear.

Just trust.

I stand there, my heart pounding, his hand now heavy and slack in mine. The T-shirt rises and falls gently with his breathing, and I'm shaken by the terrible calm of it—by how easily he trusts the world to return him to himself. To carry him to where he needs to go—and bring him back.

And I understand, dimly and unwillingly, that this was never about teeth at all.

It's about trust.

Not courage. Not bravado.

But faith—that whatever carries you away will also bring you back.

6

————

I woke up then.

Not with the groggy, half-out-of-it surrealism that the Brendan in my dream must've experienced when he came to, but with wide-open panic and a pounding heart. My mind had experienced what my body—still in the same bed, still in that same ugly, godawful immobilization brace with the white dog hairs caught in the Velcro—had not.

It had been a dream.

Nothing more.

It had come from boredom and longing and grief, and everything else I'd been having to deal with in this awful year.

I remember turning over and trying to get back to sleep, trying to slip back into it—the dream—so I could be with Brendan again. Not just my character, but something closer to a guide. More than that; a wise and kind teacher. Someone who had known about what it meant to trust the author, even when things looked bleak.

But I was awake now.

The steady hum of the air conditioner droned on while the world—lucky thing that it was—continued outside without me. Nothing had changed. My leg was still broken.

Mom and Maisie were still dead. Outside, the day went on its indifferent way—someone taking a walk up the street with a baby carriage, someone else mowing a lawn, the dogs barking in the other room at a squirrel perched shamelessly on the bird feeder.

Ordinary life that I could no longer be a part of.

The hopelessness came rushing back in.

Desperately, I tried to cling to the dream.

Brendan trusted himself to the process, willingly surrendering to a descent into darkness—just to show me what trust looked like. But as with even the most vivid dreams—and this one had been vivid—the details were already slipping away. I could no longer remember the exact shade of his amber eyes, only the warmth in them. I could no longer picture precisely how his muscles shifted beneath the T-shirt, only the charged stillness of the women in the shop watching him.

Time passed without my noticing. The light outside the windows thinned, softened, slipped away. Eventually the air conditioner won, and the dream—no matter how hard I tried to hold it—thinned, weakened, and slid through my fingers like air.

I reached down, steadied the brace, careful of the meniscal tear as I twisted, and reached for my phone.

Outside, the night was black. Crickets sang. Somewhere in the distance, a freight train moved through Haverhill in the darkness.

Three thousand miles away, at Shannon, a controller was hailing high-altitude planes nearing the end of their long journeys across the northern Atlantic. I clicked open the ATC app, set the phone down, and waited for the radio transmissions to crackle to life.

There—that voice.

Not the same, but close enough.

Oddly soothed, I let my eyes close.

Because there was nothing else to do.

7

―――――

It was 1991, and my first novel had just been accepted for publication by Avon Books in New York. I'd signed a two-book contract.

Pirate In My Arms—a title I hated, but marketing always wins—was a fictionalized retelling of the real-life tragedy of the pirate ship *Whydah* and her captain, "Black" Sam Bellamy. She wrecked off the outer reaches of Cape Cod as he sailed home with a fabulous treasure meant for the woman he loved.

The book was a success, and my publisher wanted another.

In those days, I didn't know if I wanted to be an author or an artist. Arguably, I was better at the one than the other, but I still enjoyed painting and was taking portrait painting classes in Haverhill with a guy named Mark. He was a free spirit—talented, accomplished—and we'd sit up in his studio during my one-on-one lessons—me trying (usually without success) to bring life out of the paint, he offering gentle guidance while his stereo blasted in the background.

It was largely Irish folk music—Tommy Makem and the Clancy Brothers were his favorites. During one painting session, when I was telling him about having to write another book but being lost for a character name, over the speakers came Makem's song about the early Irish saint—Brendan the Navigator.

It was my first meeting with a Brendan of any sort, really, and I didn't know at the time how pivotal that moment was, how critical the name (and its incarnations) would become over the decades that followed. The Saint. The book character. My dog. Even an Aer Lingus 757 that helped get me over my fear of flying.

But I digress.

The song caught my interest. It told the tale of Brendan of Clonfert, also known as the Navigator, a sixth-century Irish abbot who, accompanied by a small handful of monks, set out in a little curragh on a dangerous journey of faith and exploration, trusting in his own author—God.

It's quite possible that he even reached North America. Columbus himself, who won fame for that very accomplishment hundreds of years later, studied the Saint's journey before setting off on his own great feat of exploration.

Brendan.

What a great name.

And so I borrowed it for my next character, and wrote a rather zany, over-the-top, faintly outrageous sexy romp about a brilliant Anglo-Irish Royal Navy flag captain who, betrayed by a jealous fellow officer, switches sides to become a privateer for Revolutionary America, operating out of Newburyport, Massachusetts.

Brendan was a joy to write; I tossed him into the chaos of a lively, eccentric cast—something like a maritime version of *Schitt's Creek*, long before that show ever existed—and ran with it.

The woman I gave him, Mira, was also a seafarer, a tomboy with a scheming mind, a penchant for colorful language, and a love for cats. Nineteen books later, she's still my favorite female character.

If I were to write that same book today, I'd probably handle it very differently. My energy and wisdom at sixty-three are not what they were at twenty-eight. Parts of the book are ridiculous. Some things were impossible. There were technical errors and plot holes.

But it was only my second novel and I was still learning my craft.

Brendan appeared in other books—in a novella as a young Royal Navy captain, as a supporting character in the fifth novel of my de Montforte saga. He was there in *My Lady Pirate*, when he finally found his fierce and wayward daughter, Maeve, with the help of Lord Nelson after she'd spent the previous seven years terrorizing the Caribbean as the Pirate Queen of the Caribbean—a vocation that ended when Admiral Sir Graham Falconer won her heart.

I loved Brendan as a character like none other I have ever known.

And in 2013, I let him die.

I stayed with him when I watched him turn the mortally wounded, sinking *Kestrel* to point her jib-boom toward a Newburyport she would never see again, as that last sunset lit up the sky in an empty sea two hundred and fifty miles north of Puerto Rico.

I stayed with him as he walked solemnly down into *Kestrel*'s cabin to be with his beloved Mira, who was dying.

I stayed with him—and left sometime between when he wrapped his arms around her stillness, affirming his promise that he would never leave her—and the water came.

I will never leave you, he'd vowed.

But *I* had left *him*.

That choice—to turn away—cost more than I understood at the time.

And why had I let him die?

Not for the shock value (unforgivable). Not to upset the reader (though it did). Not because I actually wanted to end up in an ER with a panic attack over it (yes, that really happened).

But because I wanted him and the two women he loved most in this world—Mira and his schooner *Kestrel*, both of whom loved him back—to have an ending that would unite the three of them throughout eternity.

I wrote what I saw. I always do. I don't control the writing, or it runs up against a hard wall and stops dead. I can't force scenes that aren't there; I simply see what I see and chase them with words.

And what I saw was this: his son Connor, reckless, angry, and out to prove himself the equal of his legendary father, ignoring Brendan's wise advice and sending *Kestrel* up against a larger ship full of ruthless pirates. Brendan, distracted, in his sixties now, his attention caught between the deck he once commanded and the cabin below, where Mira was succumbing to malaria.

He saved everyone else.

After seeing the crew off in one overcrowded lifeboat, he saluted the deck, laid his tricorn on the binnacle, and went below to be with Mira as *Kestrel* went down.

And that's where I got off the ship myself, not staying to watch his end.

I left him with his arms wrapped around her lifeless body, vowing that he would never leave her.

I wrote that the water came.

And then I turned away.

He did not leave her.

But I left him.

I had a morally good reason. I'm not a voyeur, and there are moments when witnessing becomes a violation. This was one of them.

I could not stay to see what followed. I could not stay to see him drown. I could not watch his final moments, could not bear to imagine *Kestrel* slipping beneath the surface of that dying sunset and carrying him and Mira down into eighteen thousand feet of eternal darkness.

And yet, I did not yet understand the cost of that choice.

What haunted me afterward was not what I had written —but what I had not.

I received the emails. I read the reviews. Readers were furious. They had invested years in him. He was a romance hero. You're not supposed to kill a romance hero.

And because I would not show what I could not bear to see, they imagined it for themselves.

And so did I.

Drowning.

The ending itself was, I still believe, right. Three lives entwined over decades, choosing one another to the end. There would be no lonely survivor. No fraction of devotion. Mira. Brendan. *Kestrel.*

Together.

But the unanswered question—the one I refused to look at—haunted me.

I didn't stay.

And in not staying, I let imagination do what it always does when left alone in the dark.

I wish I could have seen it differently.

I am grateful now that I did not see it at all.

8

———

The following morning, the dream was only a ghost of fragments—more of a residual ache than anything visual—and it continued to fade over the days that followed. Another visit with my orthopedic doctor. More X-rays. The fracture was healing, but another four or five weeks of non-weight-bearing misery lay before me.

Two thoughts occupied me.

The first was the unavoidable aftermath of a parent's death: the practical wreckage left behind when you are named Executrix and can't actually do a damned thing. I was alternating between a walker, a wheelchair, and crutches, and Mom's house was two hundred years old—uneven terrain both inside and out, impossible for a body already made fragile by injury to negotiate safely. I was in no shape to clean out dressers and drawers, to sort through a lifetime of my mother's belongings even if I *could* get inside. And I was being pressured by my sister to do that.

Emotionally, I wasn't ready, either.

But things had to be done.

And then there was the other anxiety, pressing harder on me every day as the summer progressed.

The Oasis tickets.

We lived in England when the Gallaghers hit it big and the whole Britpop movement exploded; Fox FM, the Oxford station I listened to, joined the rest of British radio in creating a manufactured war between Oasis and Blur. Fun days.

I loved them both.

Still do.

I never did get to see Oasis while we lived in the UK, and eventually they split in an inevitable, very public fracture. I kept playing their albums, followed their solo careers, and I'll admit it—I'm a Liam girl. When a jubilant world learned that they were reuniting for a tour, and tickets went on sale in the fall of 2024, I waited on hold with Ticketmaster, heart pounding, hoping I'd be one of the lucky ones.

I was.

I spent a small fortune on three seats in Section 139 at MetLife Stadium, a four-hour drive down from Mass-achusetts on a good day. Our daughter and her boyfriend would go with me; I couldn't wait.

Of course, Tilley and Bradford—fighting over that piece of chicken meant for their dying mother, Maisie—had other plans for me.

And as each intolerable day on crutches passed, my body healed—but not fast enough. The concert date, August 31, 2025, crept closer and closer. Would my leg be strong enough? Was there anything I could do to rush it, to make a broken body hold steady in a raucous stadium crowd that, by all accounts, would include thrown beer, flying urine, fights, and worse?

It weighed on me.

Heal, heal, heal.

Get Mom's house cleaned out so it could be sold before winter.

Would I be able to go to the concert? Safely?

The weeks crept by. I slept without the brace sometimes now, kept it on religiously during the day, and always, *always*, when around the dogs. I sat in a chair and sorted through plastic bags that Chris brought back from Mom's house: bills, photos, tax records, a journal that made me cry.

In late July, still non-weight-bearing, I finally managed to get inside her house with help. I sat there in the heavy silence of her life.

I cried then, too.

Hard.

And began to do what little I physically could.

The days were awful—finding an auctioneer to sell off her antiques, paying remaining bills, shutting off services, dealing with lawyers, realtors, and a relative whose behavior broke my heart. Six weeks after the injury, Dr. Z finally gave me the green light to start weight-bearing; the fracture had healed enough that the leg needed to be brought back online. He wrote a script for physical therapy.

Life was inching forward.

I could drive again. I no longer needed the wheelchair. I still couldn't walk far; my quads and supportive muscles were weak, the joint unstable, but I could move. I could make progress on Mom's house.

Slowly.

Too slowly.

The days passed. Oasis was touring the UK now, to thunderous acclaim.

August came. They were in Canada.

They would be here soon.

August 31 was ready for Oasis.

But was I ready for August 31?

9

———

It's an ordinary day—well, as ordinary as recovering from a tibial plateau fracture and working through the death of your mother and dog all within two weeks of each other can ever be—and I'm doing my home physical therapy. I've got a yoga strap in my hands and I'm working on a leg stretch, and in my boredom I'm looking at, and through, the icon of St. Brendan the Navigator mounted on the wall above the couch.

There's a sudden loud knock on the front door. All three dogs do what they always do on those rare occasions.

They go nuts.

Brendan sails off the bed, the barrage of barking already exiting his open mouth before his feet even hit the floor; in the kitchen, behind the gate that separates them from Brendan (who despises and would happily kill them both), both Tilley and Bradford are barking their heads off.

I'm annoyed.

I'm doing my exercises. I don't want to be bothered by a deliveryman or someone trying to sell something. I don't want to be bothered by anyone or anything—not now, not this afternoon, not tomorrow—because I've already been bothered freaking enough by this year alone, and I just... really...want to lie on my bed and do my PT.

Bang bang bang.

Fuck.

I get up, pass the couch, the icon of St. Brendan, and head slowly to the hall. Our house was built in 1900, and the front door is a big, solid, heavy wooden thing with a square pane of window glass at the top, which in turn is covered by a sheer white cotton curtain. I can see three shapes beyond the curtain, no details, just an impression of height and mass. Jehovah's Witnesses, probably. But then my anxious mind is on alert; oh my God, something has happened to Chris, and the cops are outside, coming to tell me more devastating news in this summer that's had its fill of it. My irritation at being interrupted is now full-fledged panic.

I grab Brendan's collar, flick over the deadbolt, and grasping the old brass knob, open the door.

There are three guys out there.

And they're definitely not the Jehovah's Witnesses.

One is about sixty, with a full head of greying hair laced with what looks to have been some sort of red back when he was young. Not salt and pepper, but salt and deep auburn.

The other two are about half his age. One is clearly his mirror, save for eye color and small differences in the face. The third carries the older man's features and eye color—a rich, deep caramel—but his hair is thick, glossy, and colored like Nestlé's dark chocolate, flopping over his forehead in a way that, if I were a young, unmarried woman, would make me want to reach out and touch it just to put it back. There's a barely noticeable spray of freckles over his nose.

All three are obvious reenactors. And why wouldn't they be? We just celebrated the 250th anniversary of the battles of Lexington and Concord.

Brendan is straining at his collar as I crack open the door the barest inch. Who they are, and what they want, I don't know. I'm just glad they're not the cops coming with more bad news.

Actually, I don't know what to think.

Curiosity is warring with irritation, as well as something deep and unsettling that I can't name.

Do they have something to do with the state's celebrations? Did someone send them as a joke just to rattle me— some internet prank? A bunch of weirdos who know I'm a romance novelist and are taking psychological warfare to a new level by impersonating period characters?

I put my mouth against the crack in the screen door as I push it just the smallest bit open. I'm helplessly aware that any one of them—let alone all three—could yank the door out of the hands of an older woman with a recently broken leg and come in and rob me blind.

Or worse.

I take some small comfort from Brendan, whose hackles are up. He's growling and getting harder to hold onto with my unsteady leg. Maybe I should put him behind the gate. But if I do, and these nut-jobs wish me harm, I'm on my own.

"Can I help you?"

The younger one with the curling reddish-brown hair is the first to speak. "We've come to see Danelle."

Brendan is trying to squeeze through the door. He's no longer barking, just putting his full seventy-odd pounds into the collar and trying to muscle his way outside to check out the three strangers. His nostrils are quivering—sniffing, putting information together. His hackles fall back down now, his ears dropping on his head, his eyes losing their guarded look.

And now his tail...it's wagging.

As if he knows them.

"What are you trying to sell?"

The three of them exchange looks. The two younger men look genuinely confused, though the auburn-haired one carries himself with an easy, natural confidence that stands in direct contrast to the dark-haired man beside him, who seems nervous at best, dreadfully uncomfortable at worst. He's shy; not a good trait in a salesperson. He must be a trainee, out of his depth, likely better suited to another vocation. I see his Adam's apple bob beneath his cravat; who the hell wears clothes like this when it's eighty-five degrees outside?

Only the older man—who I assume must be their father, given the resemblance—seems quietly amused. His eyes are warm, sparkling; they look familiar, though I can't place them. In fact, there's something disturbingly familiar about all three of them—and the fact that I can't put my finger on it is unsettling.

My heartbeat is starting to pick up.

Again, their confused looks.

"Sell?"

I'm getting nervous now. "Look, I'm rather busy. If you want to email or send me something about your product, fine—I'll check it out. But I'm not interested in any gimmicky sales pitch, whether it's the History Channel, Boston Magazine, or whatever it is you're hawking."

The two younger men look at each other again, the confident one's brows pulling together over the bridge of his nose. The one with the Hershey's chocolate–colored hair looks even more confused. At the edge of the group, the oldest man's mouth twitches faintly at the corner. Why he finds this so damned funny is rattling me.

I shut the door in their faces, immediately throwing the deadbolt and leaning my back against the old wood. The brass doorknob presses into my hip. Something is rising in me. A hysteria. Like being trapped in worsening turbulence on a transatlantic flight. I'm in this. I can't control this. I don't know what's happening, but something's happening, and I'm scared.

Brendan is looking up at me, his eyes holding an expression I can't read.

I place a hand over my pounding heart, turn my head to the side so I can look out the veiled window, and I can see that they haven't moved. Their tall shadows are still out there, beyond the gauzy white curtain, beyond the smell of sunbaked old wood and red paint.

My heart is now galloping.

You know exactly who these three are.

And if you're right, it proves that this summer has finally broken you.

My skin feels hot. Clammy. I feel my pulse beating in my throat. Finally, the shadows behind the door lessen. I hear their clomping footsteps moving down the wooden steps of the porch, and let out my breath on a huge, shaky sigh.

I put my hands over my eyes, and wipe my palms down my face. Anchor my hand in Brendan's collar. He's very still, now, ears weighted down by gravity, almost deflated.

I head back into the living room where my bed currently lives, pick up the yoga strap and settle back. But my heart is still pounding, and I turn over and lift the drawn shade just the smallest bit. I expect them to be gone. I hope they're gone. And if they're not, I expect to see them walking up the street, or getting into a car, or heading down to the next neighbor to sell whatever it is they're pushing, but no. The three of them are sitting in a loose circle on the lawn just beyond the porch. The older one's back is to me; I can't see his face, but it strikes me that he's maybe not reenacting the state's 250th, because his clothes look a little later; the other two's do as well, for that matter. Whatever. The auburn-haired one is lying back on his elbows in the grass, knees bent, staring up at the sky and clearly taking pleasure in the summer day. The younger one looks…just lost.

The phone rings.

It's Mary, across the street.

"Danelle, there are three strange men sitting on your lawn, did you know that?"

"Yeah."

"I've called 911. I don't like how they're just sitting out there. Who are they, do you know?"

"I've no idea."

Yes, you do.

"I was walking by the window and saw them, and thought, 'that doesn't look right.'"

"No...it doesn't."

"Did you lock your door?"

Yes.

My skin is sprouting sweat and I'm now feeling faintly nauseous. I'm dreaming. I have to be. It's a better explanation than anything else, and certainly far more palatable than insanity.

But I'm driving my fingernails deep into the skin of my forearm, leaving angry red dents, and it hurts. This is no dream. And there's the sound of an engine now, and I tip up the shade a little again, to look out, and there's a cruiser out there, parked in the street next to the mailbox. The three men haven't moved. One of them, the auburn-haired swaggery one, is looking up into the sky, pointing at something; I follow his gaze. It's just a jet cruising through the stratosphere at 35,000 feet, oblivious to the utter impossibility of what's going on seven miles below it, just as the man pointing up at it is probably thinking that it, this odd thing streaking through the sky, is just as utterly impossible as the occupants of the plane would find him.

I know this.

I can't say it.

Because now I've got only two choices—impossible, or insane.

The cop is getting out of his cruiser. He's young. Hair cut brutally short. His radio and gun belt weigh him down as he stalks across the lawn.

The men haven't moved. All are regarding him with mild curiosity.

Shit.

I can't stay in here.

I know Mary's probably also peering out from behind a slitted curtain, and if the cop is now here, it's safe to go outside.

I head out and stay on the porch as he starts questioning them.

All three have gotten to their feet. Did one of them—did all of them—just...*bow*? What the fuck? No, they're not selling anything, I hear them say. The oldest one's speaking in a low murmur; there's an accent I've heard before, and the cop is handling this with restraint. He glances up at me, and I see him make a little circle next to his temple with his finger. Whatever they're saying to him, they're insistent. I don't like the tension building between the cop and the one with the swagger, and I'm overtaken, inexplicably, by an urge to protect them.

I walk sideways down the three stairs, one at a time, bent over to touch my fingers to the sun-warmed wooden steps. I'm afraid of falling, and as I descend, the oldest one turns and looks at me. His eyes are still warm with humor, even while Mr. Swagger, still engaged with the cop, looks like he's about to get combative, and the younger one's just looking like he wants to melt into the grass at his booted feet.

"Do you know these three people, ma'm?" the cop asks.

I shake my head. It's the only answer that feels survivable.

"They say they know you."

The world narrows. I stand there, blinking. Sound goes thin and distant, like it does just before you faint. I sit down hard on the lowest step because my leg won't hold me if I don't, and because the truth—whatever it is—is pressing too close to reality. I dig my bare toes down deep into the cool summer grass at my feet, concentrating on my breathing, trying to ground myself in the feel of the earth, the good, organic, cool solid earth—in sanity.

"I—"

Nothing comes out.

The oldest of the three turns toward me, then. He moves carefully, as if he understands that suddenness would break something. His expression hasn't changed; the same warmth is there, the same calm interest, as though this were merely an interruption in a longer conversation.

"She knows who we are," he says quietly.

The officer shifts, impatient. "Sir—"

But the man doesn't argue. He doesn't raise his voice. He simply reaches for the buttons of his vest.

One by one, he undoes them.

"I've caused unnecessary harm and fear, and I apologize. I should have thought of this sooner."

He gets to the last button. The garment gapes open. He

takes it off, and holds it in one hand, his head tilted just a little to the side, the corner of his mouth lifted in an apologetic smile.

But I'm still staring at what he's wearing underneath.

It's not a linen shirt. It's not part of the reenactor get-up.

It's a blue T-shirt, the exact same one he'd found in the boutique earlier this summer.

And across the chest, in the same bold letters as when he'd bought it:

NEWBURYPORT.

10

———

They weren't just guests.

They were old friends.

And friends don't leave friends standing outside in the hot August sun—certainly not when they're wearing peacoats and vests and long sleeves.

You invite them inside and give them something cold to drink.

And once you're inside, you sit down.

And you stay sitting down.

Because if you try to stand up, it's going to be more than a healing leg that forces you back down.

I dismiss the cop—he's dubious, and I wonder what on earth Mary must be thinking because she's probably watching, still, from the window—just as I would be if the situation were reversed. My head feels like it's underwater, and it's not the ragweed allergy that torments me this time of year. Something inside me wants to let out a long, animal howl of disbelief and protest even while something fragile—oh, so fragile—wants to throw my arms around them and welcome them.

Because I have desperately needed a friend this summer.

Deep suffering and grief are a dealbreaker, aren't they?

They show you who will walk with you. They strip away the chaff, reveal essences about people you might prefer not to see in their naked truth. They plumb the depth of everything they touch—and that includes relationships.

This summer has cost me a friendship that had been close, precious, and mutual. A friend who had called me multiple times a day when she was in crisis the year before—a friend I answered the phone for, no matter the hour so she wouldn't be alone in her anxieties. But this year, it was my turn to need her.

And she disappeared.

There were token phone calls, brief and careful — the kind people make when they don't know what to say, or how to stay. When Maisie died, she wasn't there. When Mom died, there was a call or two—but no flowers, no card, no late-night check-ins like the ones I would have offered her without even thinking about it.

I gave presence.

She gave absence.

I guess I didn't matter enough to her. Or maybe I was just too "much."

And so, I learned that some people require you to make yourself smaller if you want to stay in their lives. That some people are far more comfortable taking than giving. And that when the road narrows—rutted, broken, hemmed in by weeds—they don't help you steady the wheel.

They get out of the car.

They walk back the way they came.

See ya.

Another painful loss, in a year that has held too many.

And here are these three. I don't know why they're here, but yes, I do know them, yes, they know me, and instead of abandoning me in the absolute worst season of my life, they've not only shown up—they're insisting, it seems, on staying.

I lead them into the cool darkness of the house. There's nothing ethereal or spirit-like about them. Their shoes strike the old pine floors and make sound. Tilley and Bradford bark from their crates. Brendan the dog sniffs the two younger men, but it's their father who's captured his attention; his wet nose presses eagerly into the captain's hand, and Brendan leans into the scratch behind his ear with unmistakable devotion.

All three of my visitors smell of the outdoors—of wind and salt, natural cloth, and faint male sweat. Not unpleasant. Just honest.

Anchoring them in a reality that I'm struggling to accept.

I limp toward the dining room off the kitchen addition. The table there came with us from Newburyport after Dad died—a long, double-planked piece with breadboard ends, its surface bearing the quiet testimony of two centuries: dents, scratches, patina. The mismatched chairs are from the same period from which the table—and these three men— hail. Most of them are ladderbacks with rush seats, except my favorite one, sturdy and covered in layers of old paint.

They're standing there, silent.

Brendan.

Connor—formerly known as Mr. Swagger.

Kieran.

If their presence renders me overwhelmed and speechless, my dining room has done the same to them.

I pour three glasses of water—real glass, not plastic or tin —add ice, and set them before the men. Connor's green eyes widen as he takes it all in, wonder overtaking swagger. Kieran looks deeply unsettled, suspicion and confusion darkening his gaze as it skims the granite countertops, the stove, the Bose stereo tucked beneath a cupboard. His dark hair flops over his brow, romantic and unruly.

I see again why Rosalie—if he's met her yet—once thought him insufficiently bold for a privateer captain. She was mistaken, of course. Still waters run deep. Even so, with that dark tousled hair, those deep soulful eyes, and the sensitivity in his face, he looks more poet than predator.

He's chosen the most solid of the chairs and rests his hand on the breadboard table, rubbing the wood as if needing proof that his own experience is real.

He reaches for the cold glass and flinches back.

"It's all right," I say gently. "It's just the ice."

He looks at me blankly; of course this makes no sense to him.

Both he and Connor appear absolutely exhausted.

I turn to their father; he hasn't sat. One hand rests on the back of my favorite chair—the one layered in old grey and brown paint—and he draws it out slightly.

He's offering it to me.

The fatigue in his sons' faces is the kind you see after an

overnight transatlantic flight—not just tiredness, but pain. Brendan, though, is vibrant. He looks vital. Alive.

Different.

It's not just the accents. Only Brendan's speech carries that layered music—Irish softened by years in the Navy. His sons sound like Newburyport, where they were born.

He pulls the chair out further, concern faintly puckering his brows. "Faith, lass. Give that poor knee a rest and sit down."

He offers his hand. I hesitate—afraid he'll vanish, afraid my fingers will pass through nothing. Afraid this is still a dream.

They don't.

His hand is solid. Warm. A man's hand.

"Hello, Brendan," I whisper.

The concern fades from his eyes, replaced by the gentle kindness—the warm amusement—I've known for thirty-four years.

"Hello again," he says, inclining his head as he helps me sit. His eyes are alive with humor. "I told you I'd be back before you finished worrying."

11

When you've got guests, you make them comfortable.

And I see that poor Kieran's head has fallen, his chin lying on his chest before jerking back up, his eyes blinking in startled surprise as he takes in his surroundings in that brief moment while he tries to keep them open.

My confusion at finding these three at my doorstep is mirrored in his.

Connor isn't doing much better.

Exhaustion lines his face. Every so often he gives his head a short, hard shake as he examines the Pimpernel mats on the antique table; an oddity against the familiar. He is swaying a bit, pale; I almost expect him to slap his own cheek to force himself awake.

Brendan, though, looks well-rested. Not merely for an older man, but entirely so—settled, as if the long journey had passed around him rather than through him.

"Look at these two," he says, amused. "Half my age and they can't even remain awake enough to appreciate something miraculous." He ruffles Kieran's hair, startling him; the dark head has again begun to droop, and this time, he just melts sideways a bit, eyes drifting shut once more.

"Do forgive us," Connor mutters. "Travel is always tiring."

The contrast between the younger and the older deepens, and I try, lamely, for a joke about it.

"And here I thought the youth were the ones supposed to be more energetic."

The two younger ones just look at me.

Brendan shrugs, his eyes playful. "They took a different route to get here."

This couldn't get any stranger.

And now, both young men are sinking. There's no other word for it.

"I think you two should go find a place to rest," Brendan says, with a mix of fatherly concern and high amusement; as an older person myself, I personally knew the redeeming triumph of being able to outlast someone who has it all over me on youth. Because you slowly disappear as you walk through the years, becoming irrelevant, invisible, especially to the younger generations, and every so often it's nice to be able to score a small victory—to reclaim just a bit of control against time itself.

"We have two spare bedrooms," I say, already getting to my feet—and then I realize that there's a problem.

Two spare bedrooms.

Three men.

None of them short, by any measure.

And just the two full-size antique beds upstairs. Whoever takes the Jenny Lind spool bed in the northeast bedroom is going to have to lie slightly sideways to fit.

Brendan sees my hesitation and mistakes the reason for it. "Are the stairs too much for you?"

I shake my head. "No—it's that there are three of you and only two bedrooms, and—"

"I don't need a bed," he says easily, with a shrug. "Give them to the lads."

"What?"

Even the two sons, as fatigued as they are, look confused.

"I'll not have you sleeping in a chair or on the dog couch," I say. "I'll figure this out."

Bedrooms.

For houseguests.

Because where else are they supposed to stay?

Three men in strange clothes. No credit cards. No bank accounts. No social security numbers. No driver's licenses.

No identities.

I couldn't just throw them out on the street.

Insanity, all of this.

But at this point, I'm making peace with it. They haven't gone away. This isn't the way dreams dissolve. And I might as well accept whatever this is.

It's anchored in the solidness of Brendan's hand when it touched mine; in the way Tilley and Bradford push against the wire bars of their crates, desperate to get closer; and in how Brendan—the dog—does what he always does when he likes someone: parking his rump on their shoe, hips pressed to their shin, doing that little wiggle that says, *more, please.*

More scratches.

Head petting.

Neck rubs.

Brendan the Captain is giving Brendan the Dog all three.

And his two sons are falling asleep at the table.

No matter how these friends have come to me in my summer of grief—when others had left—I owe them the same kindness. There will be time, if they are still here and this strange reality remains intact, to show them my house, a bit of my world. At the moment, they're too exhausted to appreciate it.

And too enchanted, despite their fatigue, to want to leave and miss a single bit of it.

"Good night, you two," Brendan says fondly, and he goes to the sink with his glass as I lead his sons upstairs. Despite their unseasonal clothing, both are shivering, Kieran huddling his arms around his chest; it occurs to me, only later, that air conditioning would not be a comfort to bodies accustomed to natural summer heat. I'll turn it down when I get downstairs.

I settle them with towels and toothbrushes (not for sharing, I tell them), briefly explain the sink and faucets, and tuck each one into a guest room. Later, I'll figure out where Brendan will sleep. They mumble their thanks and close their doors. Their weight settles the old floorboards; the beds squeak as they climb in. Reassured, I head back downstairs.

Surely he'd be gone.

Surely I'd wake up.

But he isn't gone. He's still standing at the sink, one hand on the lever that controls the tap—flow, temperature, everything in one gesture. I'd expected him to pour himself a glass of water and sit at the table, but no. He's pushing the lever up and down, pausing midway, pushing it to the left, making it do small circles. He slips a finger under the stream, drawing back sharply when it runs hot, pushes the lever again and watches the water spilling into the basin.

He does not know I'm watching.

And I feel my own little smile as he bends his tall frame at the waist and, one hand still playing with the tap, lifts the perforated metal plug through which the water had gone and peers down into the drain as though he might glimpse the whole hidden system beyond.

He senses me. Straightens. His face is alight with boyish delight that shaves a good decade off his already youthful appearance.

"This is quite fascinating," he says, eyes sparkling. "How lucky you are, in your time."

Good God. What would he do with the icemaker? The refrigerator? My little red Miata outside with its clutch my knee can't yet manage? What would he do with airplanes and polyester, speedboats that spout diesel fuel, a vacuum cleaner, the internet, and a coffeemaker?

"I'd forgotten," I say, amused, "that at heart, you're an engineer."

The word may be anachronistic, but he only chuckles and goes back to studying the tap. "Naval architect. Privateer. Husband. Father." He grins. "And eternally curious."

He fills his glass with filtered water. The delight on his

face—watching cold, clean abundance spill effortlessly from the spigot—is enough to erase, at least for a moment, the unbearable grief that has defined this summer.

12

———

Being an author is, in its own strange fashion, a bit like playing God.

But for me, it has never felt like that.

There's more humility in it. Less control.

I can't speak for other writers—how words come to them and manifest on a page; I don't know how their stories evolve and translate to paper.

I only know how mine always have.

I observe. I listen. I watch, and follow along with a mental notepad, seeing scenes unfold, hearing dialogue, scribbling something briefly glimpsed on the back of an envelope, a Post-it at three in the morning, or in a torrent of revelation through the keys of my laptop before it can fade. I never force anything; I just watch and listen and try to keep up—because when I do try to force something, it stops dead.

It's as if the process itself knows that some things cannot be imposed.

That "organic" isn't just something you find in the produce aisle of the local supermarket.

I'm thinking of all this as I watch Brendan carry his water glass back to the table, and I realize—slowly, reluctantly—that while I might have *created* him, I've gotten some things wrong about him.

Perhaps he thinks of me as all-knowing. To him, I am the unseen hand, the force he can't question. Of course he would think I'm the one with control.

If only he knew how little control I've ever had.

It's him, all along.

He is the one who will make the decision to step forward when things narrow—to go below with Mira when the deck is no longer his.

Created.

How arrogant that word sounds now.

Because I don't create them. I come to know them. I tell their stories. But just as you might speak to a stranger on the phone, you don't know the shape of their nose, the smell of their skin, the thoughts they keep to themselves. You might exchange letters or emails for years, build a rich inner picture of someone—and then finally meet them, only to discover they're shorter than you imagined, or heavier, or their breath smells faintly of garlic.

The little things.

And I'm learning, as I watch Brendan—no longer a character I "created," but a living, breathing presence across from me—that like anyone glimpsed from afar, he has more to reveal. Things I could never have known without meeting him here, like this.

I only knew him briefly as an older man before I let him die in the shipwreck (or rather, before Connor's choice set the end in motion), and suddenly I wonder:

Is this why he's here?

For me to intervene?

For me to have one more chance to save him?

When he'd come to me in the dream some weeks back, it was as his younger self.

This is not the younger Brendan.

This is the older one, moving steadily toward his end.

How close that end is, I don't yet know.

He is somewhat different than I'd imagined him. As an older man, the easy performative charm of youth has been tempered by maturity—by the quiet weight of living long enough to lose things that mattered. Loss. Death. Children grown and gone. Institutions that once shaped you falling away.

He carries that weight without bitterness or urgency; it's just part of who he is.

And he's still curious. Still delighted by small things. The mechanics of a faucet. The question of where the water goes.

Standing next to him—especially having lost two precious inches of height myself to osteoporosis and arthritis —he is startlingly tall. Well over six feet. I have to look up slightly when I speak to him. I tell myself that nothing about him has changed since I first imagined him in that artist's studio with Tommy Makem singing through the speakers.

The truth is, I simply missed things.

Like how the fine lines fanning out from the corners of his eyes don't age him; they soften him. Warm him. Make him approachable in a way that feels almost...deliberate. His lips are shaped differently than I imagined. His nose as well. I wonder—without asking—if the starburst scar from when Richard Crichton shot him still marks his chest. If the lash marks from Crichton's rage remain across his back.

Some things deserve privacy.

And I wonder if he carries sorrow for how the Royal Navy shaped him—and then abandoned him. Or if he ever did. It certainly wasn't there when he resurfaced years later as an American privateer in 1778, and I truly met him for the first time.

Because yes—Brendan understands abandonment.

Whether it's an institution that once defined you, or a friend who cannot tolerate your pain, abandonment does not change with centuries.

He sits across from me now, looking out into the back yard. At the ash and oak trees shading the paddock where Ben Azi dozes, flicking his grey tail. At sparrows jostling at the feeder. A mourning dove pecking beneath it. The sky rises big and blue and hazy above the treetops, and a single cloud sails across the zenith.

His attention is gentle. Unhurried.

He asks about the house. The land. Where Chris is. And hearing little Bono crowing, how many chickens we keep.

And still, he does not seem tired.

Not even a little.

Something in me notes this—and quietly sets it aside.

Eventually he grows silent.

"This must be disarming for you," he says at last. "I hope our arrival has not come as too great a shock."

"Just another jolt after a hellish summer," I say, sighing. "But unlike everything else this year, your being here is a shock in a *good* way."

His voice softens. "This year hasn't been very kind to you, has it?"

I feel unwanted tears well up. They are always so close these days. I just shake my head. I don't trust myself to speak.

He simply sits there, not rushing in to fill the space.

He stays.

Bradford shifts in his crate. The room settles again.

Presence.

"I'm sorry," I blurt, finally. "I got some things wrong about you."

"Wrong?"

"You think you know someone...and then you meet them."

He studies me for a moment, then lays his hand gently atop mine. "I hope I don't disappoint."

I laugh. "No, no. It's the little things. And one big thing."

He waits.

"Your accent," I finally say.

Relief flickers across his face—and then he laughs.

"And my accent is the great offense?" He gestures for me to go on—and I tell him.

In my books, his voice had been fully Irish—Connemaran, musical, and lilting. I had imagined it well enough, I thought. But this man carries England in his dialect too, shaped by years in the Royal Navy. His speech is layered. Earned. Unique.

His, and his alone.

Not mine.

I ask about Mira.

"She is well," he says simply, affection warming his eyes. "Resting."

Resting.

My pulse jumps and I feel the little palpitations in my chest, but I don't ask him what I'm afraid to hear.

"And when you speak her name," I ask carefully, "how do you say it?"

He looks surprised. "You mean you don't know?"

"I thought I did, but I want to make sure I got that right, as well."

His brows lift a fraction and laughter dances in his eyes.

"MYE-rah," he says, simply, watching my face with amusement.

The name falls out of his lips like a love song, and his eyes soften and warm at thought of her, mirroring the endearment.

I nod, absorbing this.

"I thought it was like, *Moyrra.*"

"You've the shape of it. Just let it finish. MYE-eh-rah."

Ah, there. The word just sings on his tongue. Maybe my American ear, hearing him through two hundred years, hadn't been *quite* so wrong after all. It was there, indeed. A faint echo, but true.

He seems to find this conversation amusing—or maybe

he's just glad to bring his absent wife into it. Finishing his glass of water, he stands up and heads toward the sink.

"You must be very tired," I say, thinking of how Connor and Kieran had crashed upstairs. "There's a couch in the other room if you'd like to nap. I can keep the dogs quiet."

He just smiles and shrugs. "No need," he says. He follows me down the hall and into my makeshift bedroom, because it's time to swap dogs around and let Bradford and Tilley out to have a run. I'm not going anywhere near those two without my knee safely in the brace, still back on the bed where I'd been doing my PT.

"Come on, Brendan," I say, and he looks at me reflexively before he realizes I'm talking to the dog I named after him, and laughs.

"No shortage of that name around here today," he quips.

Brendan the dog doesn't want to be left behind while the two younger ones have their turn. As the senior canine in the house—and self-appointed owner of me—he's not good at sharing. Usually, when it's time to dog-swap, he'll deploy his well-honed delaying tactics, hustling off to the sunroom so Bradford and Tilley don't get a moment alone with me. But tonight, instead of ducking away, he follows our visitor without hesitation, and I bring him into my room and put the gate up.

"And yet another Brendan!" my visitor exclaims, and following his gaze, I see he's noticed the icon of the Navigator that hangs on the wall over the couch.

"There's an airplane, too," I say in something like embarrassed defeat.

He looks at me blankly; of course he wouldn't know what an airplane is. But I'm still wondering what this visit is about, and how he got here, and unable to contain my curiosity a moment longer, I finally blurt out my question.

The one that's been hovering all along.

"You know, I'm really delighted to see you, and to meet Connor and Kieran, but you haven't told me why you came."

"Why, you needed someone to sit with you," he says, simply.

"And how did you get here?" I don't bring up the phrase "time travel," because he'd likely give me the same blank look he did when I spoke of an airplane.

He glances a last time at the icon of the Irish saint. "Ah, well, I have friends in high places," he says cheerfully, and accompanies me back out to the kitchen as my old dog whines in complaint behind us. He's a true gentleman, measuring his stride to my halting steps, ready to help if the leg goes out on me.

"I'm sorry," I say. "I wish I weren't so laid up." I sit, strap the brace on, and carefully bring Tilley out first; she's pulling madly, choking and gagging against my hold, and Brendan calmly reaches down and takes her collar. I gratefully relinquish her; I don't have the strength to hold her back, and I don't need another fall.

He says something to her in Irish.

I have no idea what it is, or what it means, but Tilley

seems to understand him because now she's stilled, and she's looking up at him with happy eyes and a canine smile, her white tail wagging.

"Where does she go?" he asks.

"The back door, there, that leads out into the patio and back yard."

Tilley has settled right down for him, no longer putting the C in Crazy, and calmly leads him to the door. He opens it, and she shoots out into the back yard like she's been expelled from a gun, plumes of fine sand spurting up from her feet as she charges towards the distant fence.

"And how long before you're fully recovered?" he asks, coming back into the kitchen where I'm leaning against the counter.

"Not soon enough." I sigh, watching Tilley doing her best racehorse imitation along the fenceline, a white streak appearing and disappearing behind the trees. "I've got tickets to go see Oasis this weekend…I've been waiting years for them to get back together, but this leg…I'm not sure it's wise to go, at this point."

He stares at me without comprehension.

"They're a rock band," I explain.

He just looks at me, brow furrowing.

"A—what?"

I laugh and give him a primer on modern music. I explain about the Gallagher brothers—how they'd had a massive fight, broken up years back, and now have this global reunion tour. It's a once-in-a-lifetime thing. Something I wanted to see so, so badly. And now, it, too, might be a casualty of this dreadful summer.

His eyes look sad, as though he's absorbed my pain and taken it on himself.

"This event means a lot to you."

"It does. But I still have a couple of days to decide, one way or another." If I don't change the subject, his empathy is going to undo me. "And now, I'm afraid I've got to ask your forgiveness a second time, because you're a guest, and I haven't even offered you tea."

That brightens him right back up.

"Faith, I thought you'd never ask!"

I remember his fascination with the faucet. "Would you like me to show you how to make it, yourself? Though tea itself hasn't changed since your time, the way we go about preparing it certainly has."

He takes a deep breath, happy again. Tea will always be the great restorative for any Anglo-Irishman, and if he drinks as much of it as Chris does, he should be right at home. I want him to feel familiar here. I want him to like it here. I want him to stay, as long as he can.

Because this year, nobody else is staying, and I'll take what I can get.

Because if he stays, he can't board *Kestrel* with Connor in command—and embark on that final voyage.

13

———

Bradford is getting restless in his crate. It's time to do another dog-swap.

Before Maisie's bladder cancer and the dogfight that took me down, Tilley and Bradford were happy littermates—not best friends, but at least running partners, and anyone familiar with the breed knows that German Shorthaired Pointers are never happier than when they're doing just that—running.

But Bradford's stitched ear has healed with a scar. The PTSD from being knocked off my feet when I tried to break up the fight is still fresh in my mind. I don't dare to put them back together, especially now that Tilley has moved up into the Queen Bitch Spot following the death of her mother. Maisie never needed to pull rank—she was their mom, and that was just the way things were.

Losses in our multi-dog household tend to upset hierarchies in a big way. Four years earlier, when Brendan's mother, Tansy, died, it had shifted then, too.

He'd decided right then and there that Bradford and Tilley were no longer to be tolerated. The fun uncle he'd been to them suddenly hated them both.

He still hates them.

This is a black hole place when it comes to our beloved animals, and nobody was leaving. So, as it is for so many breeders with multiple dogs, it's crate-and-rotate. Or separate rooms.

Brendan—the captain, not the dog—is still politely waiting for tea. There's a woodstove in the sunroom, and he glances at it, perhaps wondering how I'm going to get it fired up and going.

I read his thoughts.

Or at least, I think I do.

"We have better ways of making tea, now," I say, and I show him the electric kettle. I briefly explain electricity, point to the outlet, and tell him not to put anything, including his fingers, into the slots—only the plug, and it goes in just so. I show him how to flip the switch to "on," and explain to him that it will boil the water itself and click off when it's ready.

Tilley's waiting to come in at the back door; Bradford is softly whining.

Brendan doesn't strike me as the sort of person who needs to be waited on. I want him to be a participant here, not just a tourist. Besides, it'll be one more thing for him to explore.

I mean, if he loved the water faucet, he's going to adore the tea kettle.

I swap dogs—Bradford is less exuberant than Tilley—and return to the kitchen to find my guest stooped over and staring in fascination at the tea kettle, an electric cobalt blue now alive with hundreds of bubbles streaming up toward the surface as it nears the end of its boil cycle.

"Would you look at that!" he exclaims, delighted.

His enthusiasm is infectious.

I had gotten that part right, I think wryly.

I pull open the kitchen drawer filled with too many mugs. There's one with three of my book covers on it, including his own, *Captain Of My Heart*, sporting a rendering of the privateer *Lynx* (which looked a bit like his *Kestrel*) from a photo I'd taken of it in Gloucester a few years back, and a model that did stand-in for Captain Brendan himself.

Another failure, I think, quickly rejecting that mug.

The envisioned model had nothing on the real thing.

And the real thing is about to touch his fingers to the glowing blue glass—

I grab his hand, just in time. "Don't," I say, gently. "You'll get burned."

He inclines his head in a way that twenty-first-century people just don't; half gratitude, half recognition—full elegance.

I go back to the drawer and find a different cup. It doesn't feel right to offer him one that's got a guy on it that doesn't look like him, and a ship pretending to be his own. There's a charming "happy mug" in there with a small figurine of a cartoonish brown dog, maybe an inch high, with big googly eyes and a happy smile, glued to the bottom. I'd bought it in a Newburyport gift shop, and the dog appears as you sip your beverage and its level lowers.

I put it in front of him.

He looks at it, looks at me, looks back at the kettle.

Whatever he might be thinking, he's not telling. Or maybe he just can't think past the alluring blue light of the kettle, which now clicks off, leaving only the residual hiss of the bubbling boil.

Above the kettle is the cupboard with tea; I show him it all, and he's fascinated by the sheer amount of choice; regular tea, decaf tea (he has no concept of decaf, let alone caffeine), Earl Grey, chamomile and herbal teas for relaxation, ginger and peach for upset stomach. I can see he's overwhelmed. Such a staggering array of choice is incomprehensible for him, maybe even a bit paralyzing.

I choose my and Chris's favorite—Barry's Gold—drop a packet into the happy-dog mug, and picking up the kettle, pour the boiling water over the bag. It steams upward and he smiles.

"Familiarity," he murmurs. "Despite the trivial matter of my accent, you know me better than you think."

"I'm married to an Englishman," I return. "Tea isn't a treat. It's a necessary food group."

He laughs, though I'm not sure he quite gets the joke.

Bradford is being polite. He sniffs my visitor, registering things about him that I can never know. Off in the other room, Brendan the dog is whining in protest, and I bring him his noon-time biscuit. Tilley's and Bradford's, too. And when I turn, Bradford's deep brown eyes are gazing up at Brendan, who's now leaning against the counter while he waits for his tea to brew.

And mine, too, I see; he's found a cup for me, and a tea bag, and he's looking rather perplexedly at the mug (because of course it's the one I initially rejected). I brace myself, wondering what he'll say; his mariner's mind is undoubtedly picking apart why the ship portrayed on it can't do stand-in duty for *Kestrel,* and oh, dear, what must he think of the model that's supposed to be him?

He lifts his eyes to mine, and one of his brows raises slightly; I meet his gaze and we both laugh. Upstairs, the floor creaks a bit as someone rolls over in bed, and I hear footsteps walking to the bathroom. I forget about the mugs as faint alarm rolls over me. There are dangers up there that an early nineteenth-century privateer might find lethal. Like the wall sockets. Hair products that smell like fruit but aren't meant to be eaten. *Shit.* Did I explain how to use the toilet? The sink? Toilet paper?

Shit.

"They're all right," Brendan says, correctly noting the alarm in my face. "You worry too much. Maybe we should make some tea for them as well?"

"You go ahead and do just that," I say, not only because I need to make yet another dog swap or think that either of his sons will be coming downstairs anytime soon—but because I know that Captain Brendan is just itching to turn on the kettle again, feel the satisfying snap of the switch beneath his forefinger, and watch the bubbles dance and shimmy their way toward the surface in their magical electric-blue light.

14

———

In 1994, Chris and I found each other across an ocean.

I was living in central Massachusetts; he was just outside Oxford, England. We met through an international pen-pal list—emails first, then phone calls—and somehow, improbably, that small thread stretched across three thousand miles and held.

By Labor Day weekend, he had come to visit and there, with the Atlantic spread before us, proposed to me on the Newburyport side of Plum Island. A few months later, I packed up my dog, my life, and whatever courage I could muster, and moved to England on a fiancée visa.

For the most part, I loved it there. England felt familiar in ways I hadn't expected—the landscape, the history—but flying back and forth was brutal for me. My imagination has never been kind. In those years, when planes seemed to fall from the sky with alarming regularity, each trip home felt like daring fate.

Eventually, it became too much.

Chris was willing to try life in the States, and we crossed the sea again, this time together. We settled in Newburyport, where we stayed until my father died in 2001, and then returned to my childhood home, where we raised our daughter and built a life that has, by any reasonable measure, been a good one.

We've been married for decades now—long enough to have crossed oceans, raised a family, buried parents, and aged into ourselves.

And now I wonder—as my inexplicable, impossible visitor watches me open the refrigerator and pull out a carton of milk—whether he'll still be here when Chris gets home from work.

He stares at the carton for a moment, then reaches out and touches it, smiling in delight at the coldness, nodding as if this, at least, makes sense.

There's been no movement from upstairs. Are Connor and Kieran still there, or have they slipped back into their own time? They're both around thirty—too old for me to go checking on them—and the not-knowing sits heavy in my chest.

Brendan turns his attention to the sugar packets—brown, white, coconut—studies them with care, then chooses the white. He tears it open neatly, pours and stirs it into his tea, and sets the spoon aside, examining it as though it's both utterly foreign and deeply familiar.

What will Chris make of him?

Outside, the late-afternoon shadows lengthen, the day sleepy and hot. There's no air conditioning here in the kitchen and dining area, and I ask Brendan if he's comfortable; he's stripped off his waistcoat and is wearing that same Newburyport T-shirt, proof that he'd been here before. His trousers are a mismatch with the shirt, in more ways than one.

If they're all still here later—if my *mind* is still here later, because right now it's certainly blown—I'll take them to Marshalls or back to that Newburyport boutique and let them pick out something more current. Maybe some sneakers, or sandals as well. The shirt tells me Brendan wants to fit in; the trousers and leather shoes suggest he doesn't quite know how.

I wash my hands and he's still watching me, afraid of missing a single thing. From the tap—with water of any temperature and force one might desire—to the liquid soap that spurts from its bottle and smells like things he'd only have known from his and Mira's Newburyport flowerbed, to the way I dry my hands—everything fascinates him. I wonder what he's thinking. Now, he's watching me reach into the refrigerator, find the package of lean ground beef, and tear off the plastic wrapping.

"Is there anything I can do to help?" he asks, whether from kindness or a desire to immerse himself in something that must feel magical to him.

"You can get me a large mixing bowl," I say, jerking my chin towards the drawer where they're kept. "And since my hands are contaminated by raw meat, you can get me some spices."

His face brightens. He's excited. He finds the bowl and sets the pink Himalayan salt, the ground pepper, the onion powder in a military line, each standing at attention, ready for duty.

Mira isn't much of a cook.

Of course he'd find this intriguing.

He watches intently as I work the ground beef with my hands, fascinated by the way it folds and yields. He adds the spices at my direction, grinning like a child watching a batch of cookies come together.

"And now the egg," I say.

He pauses.

"To bind it," I add.

He nods, solemn and attentive, and selects one from the small pile waiting on the counter. Our eggs aren't store-bought. They need a quick cleaning first.

"There's a little brush in the sink," I tell him. "Just scrub it off."

His grin spreads. This is familiar territory to him.

An egg.

Just an ordinary egg.

He picks it up, turns on the tap, and holds the egg under the running water. He's smiling. He picks up the little square bristle brush that we use for cleaning them, and steadying the egg between his fingers, begins to scrub.

In that moment, the shell gives beneath his thumb, imploding, the sharp edges piercing the bright yellow ball of yolk. He stands there staring at the egg, ruined now, dripping from his fingers into the sink. The smile is gone; in his eyes is something I can't read. He wipes his fingers on his trousers and lifts them, briefly, to his temple, as if brushing away a thought.

"Brendan," I say gently, misunderstanding. "It's just an

egg. Sometimes the shells are just fragile. There are plenty more where that one came from."

He nods, once, and suddenly sober, reaches for another egg, and something tightens in my chest.

Not fear exactly. Not yet. Just a strange, illogical sense of *nearness*—as though something invisible has edged closer without making a sound.

Startling him.

And me.

I tell myself it doesn't matter. That whatever this is, it's here now, contained within the ordinary rituals of a kitchen —raw hamburger, spices lined up like soldiers, an egg replaced by another egg.

I turn back to the bowl. To the work. To the present moment.

It won't be until after he's gone that I understand what I felt then.

Or why my body knew to be afraid before my mind ever caught up.

15

———

The moment didn't last.

It couldn't, not with Bradford begging quietly for a handout, and the utter fascination Brendan displays for the oven itself. The stove. The ordinary pot I fill with water, soon beginning to boil, just as the kettle had when I turned it on.

I pull a box of spaghetti out of the cabinet and give him the bundle of dry pasta.

He looks at it without comprehension.

"Just snap it in half," I say.

He nods, obedient, and follows my direction, dropping the pasta into the rolling water. He watches, transfixed, as the boil falters, considers, then resumes—picking up where it left off, as if nothing had interrupted it.

It's twenty minutes to six now.

Chris will be home soon.

And then I hear it...the distant growl of his black Civic, thrown down into second gear for the long coast down our dead-end street, growing louder as he approaches. Bradford clears the distance from the kitchen to the sunroom couch in one stride, nearly sending it careening into the fish tank, his tail electric, his voice loud as he stares eagerly out the window.

"Daddy's home!" I say, because I love seeing the dogs happy.

It's a special moment for them, every night. Dogs don't look out windows wondering if someone is ever *not* going to come home. They don't remember the ones who didn't. The ones you never got to say goodbye to.

They live in the moment.

Joyous.

Present.

Oh, how I wish I could.

I move to the window. Brendan comes up beside me. Together we watch Chris stop at the mailbox, pull out the post, walk up the driveway with his briefcase and thermal lunch bag. His face already registers irritation at the noise pouring out of Bradford's lungs.

Chris doesn't quite enjoy chaos the way that I do.

He likes things quiet.

Orderly.

Chris is a software engineer with a doctorate in physics. Time travel—or whatever this is—is not going to sit comfortably in his universe.

The door opens. Bradford mobs him. Chris's irritation spikes—and then he looks up and stops short.

"Chris...this is Brendan. Brendan, my husband, Chris."

I half expect to turn and find my houseguest gone—to discover that this has all been some elaborate collapse of my mind after the worst year of my life.

But Brendan is still there.

Solid. Relaxed. Real.

He offers his hand. He's taller than Chris, and there's something in his quiet presence that evaporates my husband's annoyance. I pull Bradford away so Chris can get fully inside.

"Brendan is an old friend," I say.

It's true—and also wildly insufficient.

Chris looks at me.

"I'll explain later," I whisper.

"It's a pleasure to meet you," Brendan says, and I see Chris registers the accent—even if he can't place it.

"Brendan is staying for supper," I add, and privately to myself, *and hopefully breakfast*. "And, um...be quiet when you go upstairs. He's brought Connor and Kieran with him. They're sleeping in the guest rooms."

Chris stares at me.

He's used to the number of Brendans in my life. The saint, the dog, the airplane, the book character.

And he knows the names of the book character's sons.

Connor.

Kieran.

Only then do I notice the paper bag tucked under his arm—six Sam Adams bottlecaps peeking out over the top. He sets it on the counter as though afraid the granite might shatter along with his sense of reality.

"Well," he says carefully, "I guess it's a good thing I stopped at Harry's and bought beer."

And with that, he heads upstairs.

———

I DON'T REMEMBER MUCH about supper that night. Little things—showing Brendan how to twirl the spaghetti around his fork, and how he accidentally dumped too much Parmesan over the plate, and how he politely declined the beer that Chris had brought home and instead poured himself a cold glass of water from the tap.

The Brendan in my stories was all but allergic to alcohol, as is Kieran.

This Brendan won't touch it.

Check.

I got another thing right, I think wryly.

They speak of England then and now, Newburyport, major developments over the past two centuries. Brendan asks about how different things work: electricity, automobiles, air travel. They get along, and get along well, and why wouldn't they? Two intellectual minds, each with a quiet, grounding energy that both soothes and reassures. There is no chaos about Brendan, nothing about him that invites tension or guarding. Whether Chris is believing in this fantastical experience or just playing along, I don't ask. He is a good host. Brendan is engaging, kind, and eager to be the one to make the tea we have every night after supper.

I wish I had some chocolate chip cookies to offer him.

Connor and Kieran make a brief appearance, both looking sleep-ruffled and dazed with fatigue. They decline anything to eat, politely make their introductions (looking a bit shocked when Chris doesn't return their bows), and disappear back upstairs to bed.

Chris asks why they're so tired when Brendan is not.

Our guest just smiles and gives a little shrug. "They came by different means than I did."

After tea, we go outside onto the patio. It's dark out now, the air starting to cool. My leg is throbbing and I go inside to get my brace. When I return, the mosquitoes are coming out.

I get the bug spray.

"Here," I tell Brendan. "Hold out your arms."

He looks at the can as if it's a meteorite.

"It'll keep the mosquitoes off," I say. "They're crazy this time of the night."

"Hmm," he says, taking the can. His eyes are thoughtful. "Your time has no shortage of useful things...Mira could have used this. The mosquitoes in Barbados are just fierce."

I feel everything go cold inside me.

He is still in 1813.

I swallow hard, breaking out in a sweat despite the cooling night air.

I still have time to save him.

Because I know what comes after the mosquito bite, and—

No, I'm not going there. It's likely just an innocent remark. Isn't it?

I spritz his arms, show him how to rub the stuff along his neck and nape, his ears, and hand him the repellent so that he can spray his legs. He's intrigued by the mechanism, the system within the little can that forces the spray out against one's skin to keep the bugs away. What forces the spray out? How do people get the spray in there? He shakes it, turns the can upside down, and Chris is happy to explain.

The night settles in, as if it's an ordinary one.

Gentle. Soft. Crickets starting up out in the darkness. The scent of a neighbor's firepit. The blinking light of an airliner skating a line between the stars above, on its way to somewhere in Europe.

I think of the Oasis concert coming up this weekend.

When it's time to call it a night, I hobble back inside and offer to give up my own downstairs bed to Brendan. He simply shakes his head. He isn't tired, he says. He really doesn't require a bed anymore. If he wants to rest, there are plenty of chairs about.

I start to protest; he is gentle but firm.

I leave him in the recliner, staring with fascination at the television remote, and I understand then, or at least think I do.

Of course he doesn't look tired. He *isn't* tired. Not even a little. There's far too much here to abandon for sleep.

With a bit of help, he figures out the television and watches, blinking, as a politician gestures wildly through the screen—hands going, head tipping from side to side. Brendan furrows his brow, stares for a moment longer, and looks down at the remote with suspicion.

I have the sense he'll be up all night at this rate, anyway.

Eventually, I say goodnight.

I retire to my own sleeping quarters, favoring my leg—it doesn't like the use it's had today—and invite my old dog up onto the blankets with me.

I'm uneasy, and I don't know why.

It's a long time before I sleep.

16

———

I'm not an early riser. Night owls seldom are, and a hefty dose of menopausal insomnia doesn't help. Need someone to talk to at three in the morning? I'm your girl. Expect me to show up for an 8:30 a.m. appointment? Think again.

As usual these days, my first thought upon waking is of my mother.

My mother, who is as dead today as she was yesterday, and the day before that. She'll be dead tomorrow, too.

And the day after that.

She'll be dead for the rest of my life, and so will little Maisie, whom I never had time to grieve before her unfair loss was eclipsed by that of my mother.

I lie there for a few moments, feeling the heavy cement crush of depression—the old black dog, familiar and ever-present. I think about getting up; but then, why bother? Getting up means facing chronic back pain, the reality of my aging body, and the uncertainty of where this tibial plateau fracture nightmare is going to leave me. I turn my face back into the pillow and pull the sheets up over my eyes and immediately they blink open hard, staring at the little blue flowers that pattern the sheet before me.

That was some freaking dream I'd had last night. Time-traveling visitors. If anyone was going to visit me in my dreams, at least it could've been a real person, like my mother.

Or little May-May.

I get up, throw on a pair of shorts, and swing my stiff legs out of bed. I don't want to get up. But the dogs will need to go out, and staying in bed isn't going to change my situation any.

I stand up, testing the leg, hoping the meniscal tear doesn't send me to the floor, and with my usual morning stiffness, head out to the kitchen.

And freeze.

There, sitting on the leather sofa in the sunroom, is Brendan.

Not the dog, who I've closed off in the room I'm sleeping in, but the captain.

He looks up; he'd been there quietly, reading one of my research books he'd found in the bookcase.

I glance at the title: *Seamanship in the Age of Sail*.

"Well," I say, swaying and feeling the need to sit down. "You *are* real, then."

He has already stood up to welcome me, his eighteenth-century manners intact, and makes a deliberate show of touching his cheek, examining his palms, and looking down at his chest. His eyes are warm with boyish mischief. It's familiar, because I'd seen it when I was writing his book, and he loved to use it to disarm poor Liam and his faithful crew to devastating effectiveness when deadly situations demanded courage.

"It appears so," he says, still grinning. "Good morning."

"Good morning." I nod my chin at the book. "Any good?"

"It'll do."

"Did they get much wrong?"

He thinks for a moment, and smiles. "We write about what we know, don't we?"

"That's rather evasive."

"Far be it from me to criticize an honest work." He puts the book back on the bookshelf, exactly where he'd found it and begins to move through the room. "I've been exploring. Outside. Inside. Faith, isn't it amazing, how some things remain the same while others are simply unrecognizable."

He's looking at the brick wall against which the wood-stove sits; there's a mantle above it, topped by old brown jugs and a couple of pictures. Antique fireplace utensils lean or hang against the brick backing behind the stove. A nine-teenth-century wire toaster. An old tin candle mold. A bed warmer.

Things he would know.

But he's looking down at the woodstove, the iron quiet and cold this time of year. Running his forefinger along the hard, ridged front edge. Frowning, just a little bit, as though he's examining something that comes with a great magni-tude of discovery.

"*Kestrel*... She had a woodstove in my little cabin," he says wistfully. "Mira and I spent many hours beside it."

I shake my head, amused. "You come all this way and you're fascinated by a woodstove?"

But there's something quiet in his eyes I can't read. "Efficient now...efficient then," he murmurs, looking at the old stove almost fondly.

I'm glad he finds the ordinariness of a woodstove so intriguing. He's going to love seeing the hot water boiler downstairs in the basement. The oil tank. The baseboard heating.

There'll be time for that later.

"I hope you slept well," I say, because it looks, indeed, like he did.

He straightens up, his odd perusal of the woodstove forgotten. His fingers linger for a moment on the unyielding ridge, fall away. "Sleeping? Things in your world are far too fascinating for me to even consider it," he declares cheerfully. "In the space of several hours, I've discovered you own a boat, found something called Netflix, did some research on this Oasis-thing you're hoping to see tomorrow, brought myself up to speed on the current state of the world—funny, is it not, how countries change names throughout time although the landmass itself remains the same—and examined the pictures on your walls. You appear to like this horse. I don't know much about horses—" and then, in a private aside— "Mira tried to teach me, but was quite unsuccessful, I'm afraid—but even I can see that this is a racehorse."

"Was," I gently correct him. "Gallant Fox. From 1930."

He nods and pauses at the portraits of Tansy and Marcus as we head back toward the kitchen. "And your dogs. It's obvious that you love them very much."

I love everything in my life very much. Too much. That's

why their losses devastate me. Whether it's a dog. Whether it's my mother. Whether it's my mobility. Whether it's a friend.

I steady myself.

Whether it's you.

In the kitchen, we have a row of dog show photos and award ribbons mounted on an ancient seventeenth-century plank reclaimed from a local period house. He asks their names as we stand before each frame. Marcus. Tansy. Bradford and Tilley. Brendan, young, photographed out in Springfield on his way to his championship, our little daughter standing beside me in outgrown pink pants showing her white socks, my hair still rich and red and thick then.

Holly.

Poppy.

Roscoe.

"Maisie," he says fondly, putting two fingers to her photo, as if he can touch her through the glass. It's of her Westminster triumph: Select Bitch, 2021.

God, she was beautiful.

"Yes." A quick stab of tears, and the photo blurs behind my flooded eyes. "She was special."

"She is, indeed."

"If I keep talking about her, I'm going to cry, and I don't want to cry," I say apologetically, stuffing my grief back into the steel safe where it's been locked, deep in the dark all summer. I don't have time for grief when there are endless PT appointments to attend, a house to get cleaned out by a deadline I didn't create, an estate to settle, and invoices to be paid for a woman who will never run up a heating bill again. I don't have time for grief now, either. Or maybe, I just don't want it to interfere with this impossible morning. This... distraction from it.

"I don't want you to cry," he says softly, and he lays his hand over mine. It is warm, solid, and kind. Not many people have sat with me in my grief this year, and that simple gesture almost releases the already trembling floodgate. His voice turns cheerful. Resolved. "Besides, we've got a full day ahead of us. Breakfast to be explored, perhaps a schedule to decide upon. So much to see! Can I get you some coffee?"

I'm grateful to him for the subtle steering away from that which would've undone me.

"Did you figure out the Keurig?"

"I might have, in time, but Chris was good enough to show me how it works before he left for some errands. A fascinating bit of machinery, is it not?"

I'm just about to tell him that my morning beverage is tea, when there's a sudden commotion upstairs; the toilet flushing, uproarious laughter, and the toilet flushing again.

Connor and Kieran.

We exchange glances; this doesn't sound good, and I head for the stairs.

It's not an easy climb, and I take the weight off my healing leg by hauling myself upwards with the banister. Brendan is beside me, offering a hand, but I've got this down to a science.

The toilet is flushing again, and rich male laughter follows.

"It bloody floats!"

"And this is what counts as the head in a twenty-first century house? Damn, if we had something like this I'd be finding a way to take a shit every hour on the hour just for the fun of watching it go down the hole."

"It *didn't* go down the hole."

"Push the silver bar again."

Another flush, and Connor is howling, and I realize that some things don't change across the ages—including the male fascination with poop.

"It's gone."

"Shit."

More howls, this time self-congratulatory at their own joke.

I want to flee downstairs. I'd cast them as romance heroes, and here they are talking about...poop. For the sake of their dignity (or rather, what remains of it), I don't want to intrude, but it's too late; the bathroom door is open. Two grown men—thankfully both clothed—are staring with fascination down into the toilet bowl, Kieran with his hands on his knees, bent far over, his thick glossy poet's hair tumbling over his brow and a fascinated smile on his face, Connor already reaching for the toilet's lever before the bowl can even fill back up with water for the last flush. He glances up then, sees me—and freezes.

"Good morning," he says innocently, and blinks.

Kieran, embarrassed, steps back and looks down at the blue bathmat under his feet. I can see color flooding into his suntanned cheeks.

"What is so amusing?" Brendan asks, as if he, a man in his sixties, still has to make excuses for his grown sons.

Connor and Kieran exchange glances. The empty toilet bowl is trying desperately to fill back up, and I can see Connor's fingers itching to push the lever down again.

Kieran is turning even redder.

"Um—"

"Never mind, I'm sure we don't want to know," I say, and discreetly hand them the Glade air freshening spray. "Here." I smile to soften my next words, because Connor might be enjoying this immensely, but poor Kieran is mortified. "Use this, and then wash your hands and come on down and have some breakfast."

I see Brendan quietly look away, trying not to laugh, no doubt thinking that men acting like boys deserve to be treated like boys, because that's the exact same thing I'm thinking.

And Connor? He stares at the can as though it's worth more attention than the toilet handle, and I remember then, that he has dyslexia; he cannot read it.

But Kieran can.

"Passion Fruit...fights odors," he murmurs, pulling his eyebrows together over his expressive, toffee-colored eyes. He looks up at me. "What do you do with it?"

Brendan, well-acquainted now with mosquito spray, is eager to help. Or perhaps this is one more fascinating thing he wants to explore. "Push the button. There. At the top."

"Button?"

Connor is already reaching for the can, and the nozzle is

pointed directly at an unsuspecting Kieran. My hand slashes out to shove it away before the spray can hit him in the face and the little room is suddenly thick with the cloying scent of artificial fruit, the mist caught in a beam of eastern sunlight slanting through the window.

"My God!" Connor exclaims, the toilet momentarily forgotten, and shaking my head, I decide that telling them how the shower works can wait until after breakfast. Better yet, tell them now, and show them, too, because that's one less trip on my leg I'll have to make on the stairs. I demonstrate how it turns on and how to adjust the hot water, and lay out towels, washcloths, shampoo, and shower gel. I show them how to keep the shower liner on the inside of the bathtub so the water stays in the tub, explain the extraction fan for the steam and then, with a sense of doom, I turn and leave the three of them—because dogs are downstairs waiting to go out, and I have the sneaking suspicion that Brendan—the heroic privateer captain and naval architect— is just as eager to explore the workings of the toilet, and try to figure out what happens to a poop, as his two sons are.

I risk a glance over my shoulder as I turn the corner to make my way slowly back downstairs, and my last glimpse is of Kieran grabbing the room freshener from Connor's hand and spraying it with wild abandon, like a hissing snake that can't run out of breath, while the two of them collapse in a fit of coughing—

And Brendan, fascinated, ignoring them as he peers down into the toilet, himself.

17

What kind of breakfast do you feed three hungry privateer captains from the early nineteenth century?

Toast? Cereal? Oatmeal? Fruit?

Given Brendan's somewhat unsettling reaction to his thumb going through the eggshell yesterday, I don't think eggs should be on the menu for him, though there are plenty sitting on the counter and Chris has brought in a few more before heading off to do errands.

I hear the shower going upstairs.

Deep male voices.

More laughter.

Connor, I'm realizing, is a danger to himself, just as he was when I wrote about him in *Lord Of The Sea*. He doesn't know it, of course, because there are no terms in his day for what he suffers—ADHD. Dyslexia. Restless energy. The constant need to prove himself. Add in the fact that he runs hot—and beneath it all, the deep-rooted shame that he cannot read—and he's trouble on two legs.

He's strikingly handsome, though.

People will forgive him a lot.

Brendan comes downstairs, hair still wet; he's rubbing it

with a thick white towel and smiling in bliss. He smells good —Radox soap from the British store in Newburyport, its clean aqua scent oddly perfect for him. He folds the towel neatly and offers it to me, a polite visitor, the perfect houseguest.

"Better than the tea kettle?" I ask.

He sighs with great effect. "A perfect luxury. I enjoyed it immensely."

I can't help adding, "Better than inspecting the mechanics of a toilet?"

He has the good grace to redden just a bit, evoking Kieran's horrified reaction, and his sudden laughter is infectious. He's already pulling the happy-dog mug from the dishrack, competently finding the Barry's tea, filling up the electric kettle with clean filtered water. He is happy. With his musical Irish voice, his comments are bright, cheerful, and as much a part of morning-song as the birds outside.

Upstairs, the shower is still running.

I ignore the tightness in my chest. They're grown men, after all. If they can master an eighteenth-century sailing ship, they can manage a modern bathroom. I offer breakfast. Brendan chooses something familiar—porridge. I tip some water into a saucepan, measure out the oatmeal, put in a pinch of salt, and turn on the burner, setting a timer for ten minutes.

He watches all of this in fascination.

Upstairs, the shower is *still* going. Kieran wanders down, looking a bit displaced. He's complaining about Connor monopolizing the bathroom. I offer breakfast; toast and eggs are fine with him, and seeing I've got the brace back on my left leg, he tells me I should sit down, and that he can prepare it himself if I just tell him what to do. He's intelligent; somewhat shy (and beginning to warm up, I see), unfailingly polite, quietly charming in his own deep and sensitive way.

As he sits at the table with me, an old song drifts through my head—something by Jewel, about *"a mysterious one, with dark and careless hair, fashionably sensitive but too cool to care."*

But Kieran has never mastered the *cool* part. I doubt he ever will. His sensitivity is innate, not affected.

"Have you had anything to eat?" he asks me, his nature as kind as his father's.

"Not yet."

"Da and I will make you breakfast, then. And I'll have what you have."

I make it easy on them. Offer directions. Brendan figures out the toaster and a moment later, he's setting two slices before me. Kieran brings the jar of peanut butter and watches closely as I unscrew it and spread it thickly across the bread. I hold out the knife, still coated, and invite both of them to try it.

Curiosity overwhelms manners. Their faces light up with pure joy. A moment later, Kieran is already loading the toaster with fresh bread, while Brendan studies the jar as if it might explain something important about this century.

Upstairs, the shower is still going.

"I hope he hasn't washed down the drain," I say aloud.

Brendan's brow furrows in concern. "Is that possible?"

He's looking at me, dead serious. I laugh, and tell him that no, physics themselves have not changed, that his eldest son is perfectly safe up there (*I hope*). He can go back to enjoying his tea and the toast that he, too, is compelled to try.

"So, what shall we do today?" he asks, crunching into it and touching a paper napkin to the corner of his lips. "I think all three of us are eager to tour current Newburyport, eh, Kieran?"

He nods, too mannerly to talk through his mouthful of toast. Swallows. "Aye, Da. I wonder if our old house is still standing."

The two exchange glances and laugh.

"But first, I think we need to find something more, um, suitable for you all to wear," I murmur. "You're already standing out in ways that are going to raise eyebrows, and I'm not just talking about your clothing."

"Connor," Brendan says, with a sigh.

"Connor," Kieran repeats.

Upstairs, the shower has finally shut off. He's probably drained the hot water tank. The morning suddenly feels like it's bracing itself for an electrical storm as we wait for him to come downstairs.

The storm hits a moment later.

"I'm starving," Connor announces, and if I were a younger woman I'd be wiping as much drool off the floor as there is beneath my old dog, quietly begging for a piece of toast. He's all quick impression: thick, tousled hair the color of burnished chestnut, still damp from the shower; intelligent green eyes; swagger.

Oh yes, swagger.

It's back.

And the ADHD energy I'd seen so clearly when I followed him with my keyboard is still there, and right now, it needs feeding.

"There's eggs and toast, oatmeal, coffee, and cereal, if you would like some," I say, starting to get up, but this time it's Brendan whose hand is on my shoulder. Like Kieran, he's trying to spare my healing knee.

"Cereal?"

Of course, Connor has no idea what cereal is.

He opens the drawer I indicate, pulls out a box, and in the space of a heartbeat, his expression goes from curiosity to sheer delight. His grin is wide, reckless—a hint of the chaos to come.

"Well then," he says, eyes glinting as he straightens up to show off the cereal box as if he'd just found King Tut's treasure, and I put my head, briefly, in my hands. "Would you look at this."

Not Alpen.

Not Mini Wheats.

Not Raisin Bran or Weetabix or Special K.

Oh, no.

He's triumphantly holding up the one cereal I wish he hadn't found. The one with the red box and the cartoony, blue-uniformed character and the colors meant to attract children, sugar addicts, and vulnerable moms who are too weary to say no.

"Captain Crunch," I murmur.

And I know right then that the morning's peace is—oh my God—*not* going to last.

18

———

It doesn't take long for my sense of quiet dread to bear fruit.

Kieran shows Connor where the bowls live. The spoons. The milk. And before I can intervene, Connor triumphantly slams the cereal box onto the table before us, eyes gleaming.

You'd think he'd just taken a prize sloop.

"Captain Crunch," he announces. "For the Captain."

Kieran takes the box from him and studies the cartoon figure on the front, frowning at the absurd blue uniform.

"Who dresses like this?"

Connor snatches it back and gives him a playful shove. "Aye. Is this what your twenty-first-century captains look like?"

I do not attempt an answer.

There...isn't one.

Connor dumps cereal into the bowl, filling it to a depth that threatens to overflow. Kieran gestures to the milk. Connor nods gravely, as if being instructed in artillery, and plunges the spoon in.

He lifts it to his mouth.

Time pauses.

Yes.

God help us. This is going to end badly.

The sugar hits his tongue and his face *ignites*. Eyes wide. Breath caught. He looks at me, stunned.

"Oh."

It's the last rational word he will utter for the next hour.

He goes back in. Then again. Crunching. Talking through mouthfuls. Making sounds no grown man should make. His foot starts to bounce. Then *both* feet.

He reaches for the box again before he's finished the bowl.

Brendan, who has been observing with increasing interest, calmly reaches out and removes the box.

"Easy there, Con."

Connor freezes, spoon hovering. "Da," he says urgently, "this is like dying and waking up in heaven—with teeth. Try it. Try it, Da. Oh my God, Da—"

"I'll stick to porridge and toast."

"Kieran? Try some!"

Kieran takes one nugget. Examines it. Places it in his mouth.

Spits it immediately into a napkin.

"That's appalling," he says. "It makes my teeth hurt."

"That's what makes it *perfect!*" Connor cries, lunging for the box.

He's vibrating now, washing it down with coffee. Brendan-the-dog has positioned himself beneath the table, tracking the fallout like a professional.

Brendan quietly turns the box, studying the label.

"We should ration this."

"Da—"

"What is reduced iron?" Brendan asks mildly. "You put *metal* in your food?"

"It's a vitamin," I say helplessly. "Or a nutrient of some sort."

"A what?"

Connor is no longer sitting.

He's pacing.

"I ate too fast," he mutters, hand on his stomach.

"You ate too *much*," Kieran says. "I'm leaving before this worsens." He departs for his turn in the shower with admirable foresight.

Connor pushes the bowl away. The mound of cereal has collapsed into a sodden, golden ruin.

"I need to walk."

He begins orbiting the table.

"Why don't you go outside and throw a stick for one of the dogs?" Brendan suggests.

Connor bolts for more coffee.

I head for the refrigerator and root around on the top shelf for the Pepto.

"Here. This will help."

It won't.

The opposing Captain has already done his work.

Groaning, Connor quickly moves for the stairs, taking them three at a time. I hear the bathroom door slam, and Kieran's angry protest to get the devil out, and then a sudden, violent reckoning—plumbing, laughter, panic— and the toilet flushing again.

And again.

Brendan and I exchange a look.

He sighs, and holding the now-empty cereal carton's opened flaps between two fingers, as if its contamination might be contagious, drops it into the trash barrel.

"Another successful engagement," he murmurs.

19

They want to see Newburyport, of course.

I swap the dogs around, lock up the house, and we head outside. They're in borrowed clothing for now, and I eye them dubiously. The last thing I want is to bring reenactors who look a little too much like the real thing out into the real world and try to head off the inevitable looks and questions. Brendan's in his Newburyport T-shirt, and a borrowed pair of Chris's shorts. The other two are also in loaner T-shirts and shorts, though Connor, in a nod to the familiar, or perhaps insistent on his own mixed-century fashion, is wearing his waistcoat over the shirt.

Yes, they're going to get attention.

And it's not just because of their odd footwear; Chris's shoes don't fit them, so they're in the leather shoes they arrived in. It's because all three of them are drop-dead gorgeous—not just in face and form, but in the charismatic, easy confidence of three very successful privateer captains who have outsailed storms and enemy fire, taken what they've wanted from the sea, and dealt with far bigger threats than whatever they'll face in the modern version of their hometown.

But Kieran is oblivious to what effect his devastating

warrior-poet look might have on the modern female populace.

Brendan, kneeling down beside a front tire of the SUV, is too busy marveling at the feel of rubber tread beneath his nineteenth-century fingertips.

And Connor, chomping on the Tums I've given him and hungrily eyeing my sexy little red Miata parked a few feet away—Connor's got swagger.

Too much, really.

Don't borrow trouble, I think.

Famous last words.

We get in. Brendan's in the passenger seat, Connor directly behind him in the back where I can keep an eye on him, Kieran sitting quietly behind me. I explain seat belts, and they comply.

The engine turns over and Connor lets out a whoop.

I back out of the driveway. In the rear-view mirror, I can see Kieran clutching the door handle. Brendan's already found the button that makes the window go up and down and is putting it through its paces, studying it with a puzzled, searching intensity that is almost comical.

Connor's doing an excited little thing with his hands, gesturing wildly as I put the car in drive and head slowly up the street. I remember his longing as he'd gazed upon little Redcoat (yes, my Miata has a name). Later, I tell myself, if my healing knee will allow me to work the clutch, I'll take him for a ride with the top down, do a rollback on the hill going up the street, pop the clutch and let him feel the fun of a good ol' burnout.

I make the left turn onto the main road, and soon we're humming along at a sedate forty miles per hour. They fire questions at me like hail in a summer thunderstorm as all three of them, eyes wide with wonder, watch the houses and trees whizzing past. Behind me, Kieran is trying not to flinch as each car comes at us in the other lane at what must feel, to him, like alarming speed.

Brendan's found the switches that control the air conditioning.

The fan.

The emergency blinkers, the stereo, the vents.

And Connor has already gotten his window down. He unclips his seatbelt; now he's hanging out the window like an Irish Setter, the wind in his hair, his expression one of pure rapture.

I think about reprimanding him about the seat belt, but I don't have the heart.

We stop at Marshall's on Storey Avenue, and their first experience in a modern-day department store yields strap-on sandals for Brendan, sneakers for Kieran, and casual flip flops for Connor.

Two women browsing the tops aisle are already looking up as we pass by on our way to the back of the store.

They don't look back down.

I'm reminded of Brendan visiting the boutique in my dream, and the hushed stares of the various females in the store as he'd tried on the T-shirt, oblivious to the attention he was getting.

And now I'm seeing it repeated—times three.

Age has not diminished Brendan in any way, shape or form. Kieran's got a sensitivity and the kind of hair that makes shampoo companies famous.

And Connor is just, well—

Connor.

He knows damned well that the women are looking, and it's ramping up his energy all the more.

As we walk out of the store with our purchases, Connor swinging a bag of green, blue, and neon-yellow gummy bears meant for screaming toddlers and unsuspecting nineteenth-century privateers with full-blown ADHD, I ask the sideways question I've been trying to frame since they got here. The women's attention provides the perfect excuse to ask, because if I have the answer, maybe I can stop them from going home.

Or at least provide enough information so that different decisions will be made.

My question is innocent on the face of it. Even Brendan, as clever as he is, doesn't suss what I'm really asking.

"You have quite the effect on the fairer sex," I say playfully to Connor, meeting his eyes in the rear-view mirror as we leave the parking lot. He feigns surprise, but only for the briefest of moments before he laughs; his gesture tells me he enjoys the power of being naturally devastating, but in the next he's talking about Rhiannon, and wishing she were here to share the experience with him, and I know where his heart belongs.

The setup established, I turn in my seat and look at

Kieran. He's gazing out the window. "And Rosalie?" I ask him with false innocence. "Do you miss her?"

His eyes meet mine, and their molten depths are blank. "Rosalie who?"

It's as though the steering wheel has slammed into my heart. My mouth goes dry. My hands shake and I feel cold sweat breaking out along my spine as I apologize—*I'm sorry, I'm thinking of someone else*—and he goes back to staring out the window.

My earlier suspicion was correct.

I concentrate on the road.

It is *1813.*

And he has not met her yet.

And if he hasn't yet met her, that means that they have come from, and will presumably return to, 1813. I know that, because Kieran doesn't meet the love of his life until after Connor's fatal decision that will cost both of these young men so much.

And I suddenly put it all together.

Barbados.

Mosquitoes.

Mira, not feeling well.

The malaria that will convince Connor to take her and Brendan back home to Newburyport. The illness she will not survive.

I may not be able to help her, but there's still time to save the man who sits innocently beside me in the passenger seat, watching, with fascinated joy, the way the traffic light in front of us turns from green to bright, blazing red.

Brendan.

20

———

My mother had been a strong, proud, independent and, if I may be honest (and we dishonor the dead if we paint them as anything but what they actually were), difficult woman.

You don't get to the age of eighty-six by being weak.

Mom had lived alone in that house for almost thirty years. She didn't want, or ask for, much. But in the final two years of her life, she began the decline that took her, and as her life came closer to its inevitable end, she was forced, more and more, to depend on Chris and me.

She hated it.

That decline was a long, slow glide, seen from miles out, heading for an inevitable landing. It started with little things; her arthritis advancing such that she couldn't do stairs anymore, the hearing loss that she refused to address—too bad if the rest of us had to all but scream in order for her to hear us—her impatience with doing her bills until she finally handed them all over to me. Her increasing nervousness about driving until one day, she just didn't anymore.

Her world got smaller.

It became the comforting familiarity of Andy Griffith reruns she'd seen a hundred times. Family Feud. Her favorite talk show in the mornings. She still cooked for herself, but even that was getting harder, and she refused most food I would bring her. She lost weight. Could no longer walk to her mailbox. Needed help, now, opening jars. Stubbornly dug in. She could still feed her beloved birds. She could still care for her little rat terrier, Maggie, and my sister and I privately dreaded which of the two would go first.

One really couldn't live without the other.

In April—just four months before—Maggie was the first to go. Her little body was riddled with cancer. Our wonderful vet came out to my mom's house so that neither Mom nor Maggie would have to endure the trauma of Maggie's final moments in a clinical exam room that smelled of anesthetics and fear. Our vets always give a tranquilizer first, and then, after the drug has eased the dog down into quiet acceptance, some level of sleep, they administer the final merciful injection.

Maggie was never a brave little dog, and she screamed as the tranquilizer went in. I found the vet out in Mom's kitchen in tears, with her assistant. Sometimes that just happens.

We all wished it hadn't.

As Maggie lay in my mother's lap, the second injection was administered a few minutes later, and after goodbyes, they tenderly wrapped up the small body in a blanket and took her away to be privately cremated. I stayed for a while with Mom, but knew she wanted to be alone. Leaving her with nothing but her tears and that now-empty house was one of the hardest things I'd had to do, but her grief was a private thing.

Something never to be witnessed by others.

I found her another little dog, Henry, and she had him for eight weeks before her own sudden and unexpected end came following the fall and that visit to the emergency room.

They should never have released her.

A woman who lived by herself, frail, weak, and two weeks shy of her eighty-seventh birthday.

But they did, and it was yet another blame that I took on, myself.

I should've known.

I could have done something.

Perhaps it's human nature to milk the circumstances around anyone's death for some desperate shard of comfort, and I did. At least little Henry was with her at the end; she wasn't completely alone. But my guilt and self-blame remained. I'd been fooled by her independence, her vehement assurances that she didn't need this, didn't want that.

What could I have done differently to save her?

As I lay there in the weeks after her death, confined to a few rooms in the downstairs of the house with my fractured leg, I thought of how fiercely she had resisted almost all of the help I tried to press on her.

Meals on Wheels?

She hated them, and sent most of them home with me.

Can I do your laundry, Mom?

She allowed me to do it twice, and hid her dirty clothes in black trash bags so she wouldn't have to suffer the humiliation of her daughter seeing them, even if it was a loving attempt to help her out. She was having trouble with hygiene. Showering. She was failing, and hiding it as best she could.

"Mom, I think it's time to get some home health care in, to help you shower."

And her blue eyes would go fierce, and she'd give me *The Look* that had silenced me as a child, still effective on my adult self, and snap, "I'm not having anyone coming in here and wiping my ass!"

Okay, Mom.

And she damn well wasn't going into a nursing home, either. It was her biggest dread, and in the final weeks of her life, she put on a brave face of denial in a desperate attempt to protect her independence. She didn't tell me that she could no longer get out to her bird feeder to refill it. That just getting from one room to the other was so hard. She didn't even have the physical strength to lift a cast iron skillet —still coated with bits of hamburger and the spatula she'd used to cook it—from the oven in which I eventually found it, to the sink.

She hid so much.

And I knew why.

She couldn't face the truth. And she knew that if I found out how bad things had really gotten, I'd likely have coerced her into something she vehemently fought against, just for her safety.

Her own good.

Mom made her choices, as painful as they were for both of us, and as I sit here in the driver's seat of the Pathfinder thinking of what Kieran has just unwittingly, unknowingly revealed, I feel the same fierce instinct to jump into something that doesn't welcome my interference, and bend it to my will.

After all, I'm the author.

I can do what I want.

Right?

"Rosalie who?"

With that sentence, he'd told me all I needed to know.

21

Looking back, that day in Newburyport feels blurred around the edges. It's what happens when you try to fit too much into too little time, though I didn't understand that yet.

I didn't know how little time I would actually have with my visitors.

Or perhaps the blur came from something else entirely.

Kieran's quiet revelation still sat heavy in me, pressing at the edges of every moment that followed. The question of what to do with it—and whether anything *could* be done— rattled me enough that I didn't commit the day to memory the way I might have otherwise.

We have lunch at a seafood restaurant overlooking the harbor. The mouth of the Merrimack River opens out into the blue, blue Atlantic far out in the distance. My guests are both fascinated and a bit disgusted, I think, by the sea of fiberglass boats and their loud, stinking motors; why not use the perfectly good, honest, wind blowing in from the southeast? Why so few sails? The constant interruptions from our waitress rattle them; the massive portion sizes, when the plates are brought out, widen their eyes into shock.

Brendan has chosen a simple haddock dish. Connor goes

for fried clams, onion rings, and French fries, and I'm secretly thinking it's a good thing I've brought a roll of Tums along, as he's going to need them. Kieran sits with a cup of tomato soup and a fresh, warm roll.

There is something distant about him. As if the noise, chaos, and unending stimulation here are already too much, and he's silently retreating inward.

Not Connor, though, chomping on an onion ring and asking his father what he thinks of the lines of these shiny white craft. He laughs and points at someone in a kayak, and the sugar in his Coca Cola starts hitting his already volatile bloodstream; he's leaning back and bouncing his flip-flopped foot up and down as he casually rests his lower leg across one thigh. I've bought him a baseball cap from one of the local shops, the Red Sox's iconic "B" at the back of his head, the plastic strap across his forehead. He's copying what he sees other men in this strange time doing, and he's having a blast. If not for the waistcoat, he'd almost look like he belongs here.

An illusion that, as the day progresses, will prove how dangerously out of place he actually is.

We tour some shops, hit the Custom House Maritime Museum, where the remains of their time peer out from glass cases and framed pictures, and I feel Kieran withdrawing even further.

"There's Tracy's ship."

"Never did like the way she handled a stiff easterly. Unhandy thing, she was."

"Oh, look—this one. *Dreadnought*? Da, you ever hear of her?"

He's admiring the clipper ship's elegant lines. The greyhound of the sea, she was, a ship that made Newburyport famous in her heyday, and he can appreciate her design although he admits that she came after his time. They move through history. Old photos of Newburyport mansions built on fortunes from privateering, the triangular trade, politics, and there, in a frame on the brick wall amidst a collage of period ships—

Kestrel.

Brendan stills. Kieran is just looking at the painting. And Connor, still running on Coca Cola octane, is already bursting any restraints his nineteenth-century manners demand of him. Volume of his voice. Enthusiasm. And his words, as impulsive as everything else about him.

"Bloody *hell*, Da, look! It's her! She looks just like she did when we stepped off her yesterday in Barbados!"

People are turning and looking at him.

"Con, keep your voice down," Brendan says quietly. "Remember where we are."

Connor's peering closely at the painting, the brim of his baseball cap shielding his suntanned neck. "Who's that they painted at the tiller? It kind of looks like you, Da. Or me. Aye, it's me, I can tell just by the way he's standing—"

"It's Da," Kieran says quietly, flushing in embarrassment as a man with a camera around his neck, his presumed wife at his side in grey hair and clip-on sunglasses, regard Connor with suspicion. They exchange glances, then slowly retreat, melting back into the crowd of other visitors.

"No, it's not Da, you can see right here that it's me," Connor says loudly, and now I notice one of the employees looking up from a desk, putting a pen down, and heading our way.

"I think we should go," I murmur, and before Connor can protest further, Brendan has his son's elbow and is firmly steering him out of the brick-walled room caught in a history that will never live again, and back outside into the clean white Newburyport sunshine.

22

———

I'm happy to get out of there.

With the exception of Connor, I think we all are.

Outside, the sunlight is white-hot, bleaching away the disturbing moment and leaving me wishing I'd brought sunglasses. There's a fresh, salty breeze coming in with the tide, and I inhale it deeply.

I hope that's the worst this day is going to lend us.

And pigs will fly.

We walk the downtown area. Market Square, the boardwalk, and Newburyport's bricked sidewalks, lumpy and uneven from tree roots and frost heaves. I'm glad I'm wearing my knee brace, though it's going to be an Advil night. We duck into art galleries (Connor yawns) and specialty shops, grab coffee, make a quick trip to the American Yacht Club where I retain a membership; there, Brendan is fascinated by the keypad that unlocks the sliding gate. We head down to the docks that line the entire front of the Club's main building. The tide is already lifting them, the water banging them against the floats. A gull watches us from a nearby post. Connor's laughing again, and already moving to inspect a sailboat tied up at the dock. Brendan and Kieran join him. And why not? The shape of things may change, but the essentials remain the same.

Sea captains—and boats.

It's familiar ground, and they're comfortable here.

"Look, the rocks are still there," Kieran says, finally coming out of the embarrassed silence he's been carrying since the incident in the museum. He points to them, slowly disappearing under the rise of the tide.

"Aye, and as dangerous to the unsuspecting captain as ever," Brendan says, easing himself down into one of the wicker rocking chairs set up to overlook the harbor. Kieran wanders away, placing his elbows on the wooden railing and gazing out over the water.

I'm worried about him.

Connor has found the vending machine, and I give him a dollar so he can buy himself a drink. I'm not surprised he's thirsty; he probably consumed enough salt to melt a December driveway after his fried indulgence at lunch.

We bask in the timelessness of the moment. Brendan remarks how the jetties weren't there in his time, and how it looks like the entire mouth of the river is different, and I explain that yes, a century ago, the Army's engineers changed the river's natural mouth and redirected its path. He frowns, just a little bit; if this doesn't quite sit well with him—and I think it doesn't—he's too polite to say so.

Connor comes back, trying to figure out how to open the soda can; I show him where the thumb goes in the little ring tab, and I'm tempted to shake the hell out of the thing before handing it back to him—but he's given all of us enough excitement for the day.

I'm too old for his energy.

We don't stay long at the Club, and I sense that these three find the maritime skills of modern sailors to be a bit pretentious; when Connor starts proclaiming that nobody here knows what it's like to take a square-rigger out through the mouth of that river, or get to windward of an enemy ship to get the weather gauge and pound the daylights out of them, people are starting to look at him with a mixture of disbelief and affront.

"He did a stint as a deckhand on a tall ship," I offer lamely, covering for him. "You'll have to forgive him."

"A what?" Connor asks, frowning.

"Just stow it, Connor," Kieran snaps, and stalks off towards the gate.

Connor's now drawing himself up, taking the measure of one of the well-heeled boat owners who's regarding him with a faint curl of his lip.

Fucking asshole, the guy mouths.

"Time to leave," Brendan murmurs, once again seizing Connor's arm.

Or evacuate, I think.

We get back in the SUV and head to Plum Island airport, because if there's anything these three should experience before they depart, it's the wonder of manned flight. I check them in. Connor, the near altercation back at the Club already forgotten, is vibrating with excitement. Kieran's listening carefully to the instructions, his eyes sober.

Brendan notes how the orange windsock fills with the breeze, and asks its purpose. The forms filled out, the pilot leads us out to the field, chooses his plane, does his checks, and the three of them climb up into the Cessna.

I remain firmly on the ground, relieved that the plane can only accommodate four people.

"You're not coming?" Connor asks in disbelief from the back seat, as though I'm sacrificing something holy.

"Absolutely not," I declare. Moments later, the engine roars to life and the plane taxis away from me towards the little runway, moving far down the field. As the pilot turns it into the wind and it comes roaring toward where I stand, going faster and faster until it lifts gracefully up and into the air, I see Connor at the window, waving wildly to me, mouth open in a shout I can't hear.

I smile and shake my head.

It's a good thing Rhiannon is young.

He's a lot to manage.

23

Pumped up from the plane ride and already burning through the heart attack fest he'd inhaled at lunch, Connor is all swagger as we stop at Hodgie's on the way home.

If you know, you know. Hodgie's is a local ice cream stand, and you don't order a large because a large is seven scoops.

Yes, that's what I said.

Seven.

The sun is sinking now, and Chris has texted me to ask when we'll be home. Kieran slumps in the back seat, his eyes distant. I suspect he's already homesick. Connor and Brendan are discussing wind as it relates to flight versus sail.

Hodgie's is packed.

Long lines wait in front of the windows. College kids scoop homemade ice cream from giant freezers, and with each festive cone carried past, Connor's eyes widen. Rainbow sprinkles on mounds of frozen confection. A hot fudge sundae with a fluffy cloud of whipped cream, topped by a maraschino cherry. A woman feeds her toddler, who's kicking in his stroller, a spoonful of her banana split. The sun is still hot; one of the servers advises the boy in line just in front of us—he's ordered a chocolate chip cookie dough with rainbow jimmies—to mind the dribbles already melting down onto the sugar cone on which it's perched.

As the kid passes, Connor is staring at the cone as if it's a British merchantman ripe for the plucking.

"I want one of those," he announces, as we approach the window.

Brendan raises a brow. I'm rubbing a nonexistent itch on my forehead, wondering—in the same unhelpful way one ponders winning lottery numbers—whether Ritalin could be considered a topping option. Kieran looks faintly disgusted as the cone is handed to Connor.

Shit.

I forgot to tell him not to order the large.

Shit, shit, shit.

Connor is delighted. He doesn't quite know what to do with this towering confection; it's tall enough to be in very real danger of toppling off the cone, already melting onto his fingers.

Brendan orders a baby-size chocolate chip in a cup. Kieran, a half-size vanilla, no toppings, no sugar cone, just the ice cream. He leaves us and heads for a picnic table far away from anyone else, and something tugs in my heart for him.

He's already checking out.

Done.

And I think about how Rosalie is waiting for him in his future—Rosalie who will understand his sensitivity, his deep, deep soul, and care for it with the tenderness it deserves.

Rosalie.

I get my usual half-baby sized cone. Brendan and Connor, cocky and proud of the oversized ice cream, are flanking me. Both are naturally protective, and I've caught Brendan discreetly eyeing my leg once or twice in the last half hour. He knows it can still give out—especially as I can't hide the limp now. My own physical reserves are nearly spent.

I appreciate their chivalrous concern.

But even as I make this observation, the knee—still hurting, still unreliable—adds weight to the thought that has been stressing me all day.

The concert. It's tomorrow night.

I've waited years to see it.

Perhaps I shouldn't have taken my visitors on such a long tour of their city, knowing I'll need my energy for the concert. And even as I have the thought, I stuff it down. I wouldn't have traded today for anything.

Should I go?

Risk injury?

Push my body beyond what it can handle?

Or stay home?

I don't know what to do. There are no easy answers, and the clock is ticking.

I ponder it, out loud.

"What's Oasis?" Connor asks, managing to keep the seven scoops of ice cream firmly anchored to the hapless cone in a balancing act that a trained seal would envy. I briefly explain. Out of the corner of my eye I can see Kieran looking at him with something bordering revulsion. There are lines of fatigue around his soulful eyes. Sorrow.

I don't like how quiet he's become.

"Did you enjoy the airplane ride?" I ask him quietly.

He rouses himself from his reverie and offers a grateful smile. "I did. It was somewhat frightening, but what a treat to see the sea from such a height, and a gull's view of our little city." He smiles beneath the ache in his eyes. "Thank you for such a kind gift."

"I'm still peeved that the pilot wouldn't let Da take the controls," Connor interrupts, his tongue coming out to catch a milky river of ice cream as it races down the side of the cone.

"I am rather glad he did not," Brendan quips. "Some things are meant to merely be observed and enjoyed, especially without the knowledge of how to operate them."

"Baah," Connor says, shrugging. "You could've taught that fellow a thing or two. Any of us could have."

"Did we reach the ground safely?" Kieran asks, his voice showing a slight edge.

Connor just looks at him.

"Because if we did, I daresay we had a nice air-sail."

"Flight," Connor corrects him.

"Um...I think I'm going to go get more napkins," I say, and push myself to my feet with the aid of the table's edge. Sitting for even a few minutes has aggravated the knee, and it takes me a few steps to get the stiffness out as I head back to the counter. There's a presence beside me. Brendan. Whether it's because he can see I'm in pain, or accompanying a lady through the perceived danger of an ice cream stand parking lot is just his century's way of doing things, I don't know—but I'm grateful.

We begin to pass a picnic table with a black lab carelessly tied to one of its legs. He's no more than a puppy, maybe fourteen months or so, coat shiny in the sun, tongue lolling. He's lively, eager—just a dog being a dog—barking as people walk by with ice creams, dropping into doggie-bows, lunging up and hitting the end of the leash. His owner, a guy in his late 20s with black, short-cropped hair, is staring down at his phone, totally absorbed as he absently digs a spoon into what looks to be a hot fudge sundae.

An innocent scene.

Unless you're injured.

At that moment, the dog jumps at us, playful and energetic, and the loose slip knot beneath the seat of the picnic table gives. The full force of the dog hits me. My ice cream flies from the cone. My leg has no chance. I collapse sideways. *Oh, no.* No, God, please, don't let me break yet another bone, please, please, please—

My body never hits the ground. Brendan catches me, saving me yet another visit to the local ER and orthopedic surgeon. I have a brief, hard impression of slamming into his wiry frame, his arms around me, the breath momentarily knocked out of my lungs by his sudden catch.

"Oh my God—I'm so sorry," the man blurts, lunging for the lead. "Max! What the hell? I though he was tied—are you okay?"

"I'm fine," I say, breathing hard. Brendan lets go of my

arm but stays close, and I see him looking down at my leg, surveying it for damage. "I have three dogs of my own, so I know what—"

I don't get the chance to finish.

Connor is there.

The ice cream cone is gone, splattered on the hot gravel back near our table, forgotten, and his green eyes blaze with fire.

"You will apologize to the lady," he says hotly. "She could've been badly hurt."

"Connor, I'm fine," I say, sensing doom. "It was an accident."

The man straightens. "I *did* apologize."

"Well, I didn't hear it. This woman is under our protection and I will have your apology."

People are staring.

A few have their phones out, ready to record and make this moment go viral.

Those at the windows are turning around to look.

The man is staring at him. "You gotta problem, bro?"

"I'll give *you* a problem, *Sir*," Connor says icily, his hand going for a sword that's not there—as if muscle-memory could outrun sense. Luckily, Brendan steps between them, one hand firm against Connor's chest.

"That's enough." And then, to the man: "You have our apologies. It was an accident."

From the corner of my eye I see Kieran, his face infinitely weary, heading our way.

I reach down to pat the dog's shiny black head and send

Kieran back to the counter for some to-go containers and lids. Brendan offers his elbow and takes me back to the Pathfinder. Connor, sulking, trails behind us, and turning to check on him, I see him glaring at the offender from over his shoulder.

I'm shaking.

This cannot last. Connor is out of his element. Kieran is unravelling at the seams. Someone is going to get hurt.

We ride home in silence.

24

───────

Chris is getting supper ready when we get home and head inside—burgers for the grill. Connor's humiliation is palpable. His unmet need to defend me, an overload of sugar, and his irrepressible energy make him the human equivalent of a German Shorthaired Pointer, I think.

He can't help what he is.

My heart hurts for him.

But male pride is a funny thing, and I say nothing; instead, I offer him a nice cold can of black cherry-flavored seltzer water straight from the fridge, thinking the carbonation will amuse him.

No sugar.

Should be safe.

He makes his excuses and follows Kieran, who's already had enough, upstairs.

"What did you guys do today?" Chris asks, sprinkling salt over the ground beef patties he's arranged on a sheet of waxed paper on the kitchen counter.

I leave Brendan to fill him in, and head to the downstairs bathroom. There, the Advil. Not one. Not two.

Four.

And the ice pack from the freezer, and a short date with the sunroom recliner.

I idly flip the TV on as Chris goes outside to get the grill going, Brendan in his wake, eager to see a demonstration of this latest modern invention. I would've thought that nothing could top an airplane ride, but he appreciates every discovery with the delight of a child watching bubbles blown through a straw—curious, attentive, amused. Chris is a good teacher. I gaze at them fondly through the sunroom window. Brendan has the spatula and is placing a hamburger patty neatly down on the grill's grating.

Doesn't he ever get tired?

I'm wiped out. His sons are upstairs resting. They're half his age, young and vital. He's in his 60s.

And he's still going strong.

We eat outside under the umbrella in the evening breeze. The menu is perfect for a late August evening: Sam Adams, burgers, potato chips. Connor is enchanted by ketchup; I amuse him further by showing how you can draw a smiley face on your burger patty before sealing it with the top bun, and he laughs, his crushed spirits already restored. The sunset is hazy and red. A robin calls out a goodnight from a nearby tree. In the nestboxes mounted to the barn, the sparrows are quietly tucking themselves in. The mosquitoes are coming out, and we all go inside. Paper plates make for a quick cleanup, and Kieran offers to do what dishes remain.

Brendan makes tea for everyone, and eventually we all sit around the TV.

My leg is throbbing beneath the refreshed ice pack.

So, are you going to go to the concert tomorrow, or not?
Better make a decision, girl.

My shoulders feel like they're holding up a slab of concrete. My heart feels hollow with the realization I've been refusing to acknowledge. As if reading my mind—or simply because Chris has known and loved me for over thirty years—he's the one to say it out loud.

"Have you decided about the concert tomorrow?" he asks. "Because if you're going to go, you'll have to leave early. It'll take five hours to get down there—more with traffic. And the kids will need to know if they're going, or not."

The kids. Our daughter and her boyfriend, who aren't really Oasis fans—country is more their thing—but who are happy to drive me down to New Jersey and share in this experience I've been looking forward to for the last year...the last dozen or more years.

An experience that I know, deep in my bones, that I'm not meant to have.

I seldom make big decisions with the head—I'm a heart-kind of decision maker at my core, but the reality is undeniable, looming, and increasingly insurmountable. Five hours down, sitting in the back seat of the SUV while Devin drives. The mechanics of getting from the vast parking lot of the MetLife stadium into our seats when any extensive walking is still out of my reach? How would I manage that distance —with a wheelchair? Crutches? Can I even get a wheelchair inside and if so, where would I store it? And once we've found our seats, what about the 80,000 people, many of them inebriated, all screaming and swaying and dancing as one mighty throng to music that is no longer about songs, but anthems?

Reality is closing in. I'm alone in my indecision.

On the television, the nightly barrage of bad news yields to a local meteorologist out of Boston standing in front of a digital map of the northeast, forecasted temperatures lit up across the screen behind him.

Are you going to go or not?

Five hours down, with spinal stenosis and knees in late-stage arthritis, one of them recovering from a serious injury. Several hours at the concert, all of it standing if I want to see anything. Likely airborne urine. Thrown beer. The impossible trek back across the parking lot to the Pathfinder, where it'll likely be one big traffic jam of everyone trying to leave at once. It'll probably be another hour before we can even get out of the parking lot and onto the road. Poor Devin doing all that driving, and another four or five hours just to get home.

And something Devin had said earlier, sticks out in my mind beyond everything else.

"I'm worried about all that movement...what if someone bumps you?"

The innocent incident at the ice cream stand tells me exactly what will happen if someone bumps me. Brendan had moved quickly to catch me, but in a jam-packed stadium of moving people, one bump is all it's going to take to send me to the floor.

To reinjure my leg.

One. Little. Bump.

I can feel the hot sting of tears behind my eyes.

The forecaster has a wand, pointing at the map behind him. Through the dawning realization that I cannot go to see Oasis—to thrill to Noel's guitar and Liam's swaggering snarl—I can hear his words.

"Today's light breezes will strengthen tomorrow in the wake of a strong front that will move in overnight, and tomorrow will be a perfect summer day, with a brisk wind out of the west."

Chris is still waiting for my answer.

I just look at him and shake my head. He accepts my decision. Out of the corner of my eye I see Brendan look at me, and I know that he understands me almost as much as Chris does. And in some ways, probably better.

The meteorologist is still blaring on, and I make an attempt to watch him, to anchor his neutral TV presence against the flood of water welling up behind my eyes at the unfairness of this summer, because this is just one more loss to accept.

One more grief to absorb.

One more hit.

"Winds should be stronger nearer the coast, becoming southwest later in the day..."

I pull a tissue out of my pocket and turn my face away, discreetly dabbing at my leaking eyes, but I needn't have worried.

All three of our mariner guests are fascinated by what's on the television.

"How do they know such things, and so far in advance?" Connor asks.

"Technology," Chris says simply.

Kieran's looking quite taken aback. "Imagine how many lives could be saved if we'd had this kind of prophecy in our own time."

Brendan's doing a little thoughtful gesture involving two fingers and his chin, and there's something in his manner that is faintly reminiscent of Connor. A calculation. A plan taking shape. Something benign in its nature, but profound nonetheless.

"Imagine what a perfect day it would be for sailing," he says simply.

If only I could have known what was materializing behind his warm amber eyes.

If only...

25

Before the night has ended, I've made my decision.

I gift the precious tickets to my houseguests.

A load slides off my shoulders. No more stressing about it. No more carrying its weight. Letting them go in my place feels like the right thing to do—a way to punch back at the universe for its cruelty this summer. *Take that, Universe.* I'm going to turn my suffering on its ear and instead, choose joy in giving someone else the experience of their lives.

I feel peace about it.

A strange triumph.

It is, after all, far better to give than to receive.

Brendan declines the remaining ticket, saying he has other plans, but Connor and even Kieran are incandescent with excitement. They want a crash course in Oasis so they can fully enjoy the experience, so I lend them my iPhone, show them how to sync it to the Bose remote speaker, and pull up my extensive list of Oasis songs. I laugh, watching them. Connor is howling *Wonderwall* like he's known it forever; Kieran is already asking about what to wear, and I'm trying to figure out how to get them to New Jersey.

Trains, planes, automobiles...

The only logical option is, of course, the train. Chris

offers to drive them down to North Station in the morning so they can grab the Amtrak to New York City, spend some time there, and then take the local rail out to MetLife Stadium. We spell it all out for them, write it down, and I give Kieran the step-by-step written instructions.

I go to bed then, and cry myself to sleep. Tears of grief. Tears of relief. Tears of gratitude that I'm in a position where I can give these two such a gift, and that I can find my own joy in theirs.

And nobody hears—except the third Brendan in this strange trilogy, the canine one—watching me with dark, steady eyes from the side of the bed nearest the window, where the night air slips in, stirring the curtains.

THEY LEAVE MID-MORNING. Connor is so excited he's barely slept, and it shows. His mind has been racing all night, anticipating the train ride, the crowds, the music, the sheer joy at being alive in this century. He has no idea what a Champagne Supernova is, and neither do I, but he's eager to find out.

"I'll send texts! I'll take pictures with the burner phone you got us!"

"Wait!" I say, worried. "Do you want some earplugs?"

"Earplugs?"

Chris explains.

Connor just laughs and declares that if he can tolerate a ship's guns at close range, he's sure music will not be an issue. He's all but dancing as we move through the sunroom toward the back door. Past the framed photos of Marcus and Tansy. Past the plants in the bow windows, past the couch.

Past the silent woodstove.

His enthusiasm is infectious, almost too much this early in the morning. Chris is frowning, and I hope he can deal with such energy all the way down to Boston.

"Come, Kieran, you'll make us late!" Connor urges.

But Kieran's back at the dog crates in the kitchen, squatting down and thrusting his fingers between the bars, touching first Tilley, who leans in for a scratch, and then Bradford. Brendan the dog is behind the gate with mournful eyes, and Kieran doesn't forget him. He looks almost lost. Almost emotional. He's got the kind of eyes a woman can drown in. Rosalie will fall hard when they meet. I already know that. Because Kieran...he is special, different, in the most precious of ways.

He leaves the dogs and comes out to join us, and his eyes have a strange sheen to them.

"You don't have to go if you don't want to," I say softly, because in that moment I don't understand.

I don't know what he already senses.

"I have to," he says simply, his voice a little rough, and mustering a smile, he draws me into his powerful arms, so strong and wiry like his father's, and holds me a heartbeat longer than I expect.

"Thank you," he says quietly.

"No need to be so final, Kieran," I say. "I'll see you guys later tonight, when you get back."

We head outside. Connor is already out in the driveway, pacing, pacing, pacing.

And now he's singing loudly, obliviously happy, and I hope the neighbors are already up because if they're not, they will be shortly.

"I need to be my-sellllf, I can't be no one ellllse, I'm feeling supersonic, give me gin and tonic, you can have it all but, how much do you want it?"

Oh, dear God, he's even perfected Liam's snarling whine.

Kieran shoots Connor a long-suffering glance as he shuts the big barn door behind him. His eyes hold tenderness and fatigue—the look of someone who knows loving his brother means constant vigilance.

It's going to be a long day of managing what this century throws at him.

An even longer evening.

And Chris's face is now flat, the way it gets when he's shutting down and retreating to a quiet place in his mind. He slides into the driver's seat and the door closes with something like a slam.

I don't blame him. He's had quite enough of Connor.

We all have, I think fondly, and I love him anyway.

"Give me a hug," I say to Connor as he's about to jump into the passenger seat. He turns, lifts me off my feet in his exuberant embrace, and swings me once around before setting me gently down, making me laugh. "You're my Wonder-*waaaaal,*" he sings happily, his eyes dancing as he offers me the Gallagherian praise, and dives into the car, hand already reaching for the radio.

I lean in and give my husband a kiss and mouth a quiet *thank you*. He'll be listening to classical music on the way back from dropping them off in Boston—not as entertainment, but as medicine.

Brendan stands quietly in the driveway with me as Chris starts the car and everyone's putting on their seat belts. Behind me, the windchimes on the porch are making music.

Last night's forecaster was right.

"You sure you don't want to come with us, Da?" Connor asks. "Still have that extra ticket!"

Brendan shakes his head. "I have something important I must attend to."

26

———

We watch the Civic head up the street, hear it shift from second to third, and as I always do when a loved one departs into the great unknown, I steeple my hands to my chest, dip my lips to my fingertips, and say a prayer for their safety.

The car grows smaller, the engine noise fading. It disappears around the little bend at the top of the street. I hear the engine a final time as Chris turns onto the main road, and the day goes still and quiet, except for the wind chimes still jangling over the porch, the same few notes over and over, hitting my soul like a dirge.

They're gone.

I feel strangely empty. Something feels so...finished.

But Brendan is still standing quietly beside me.

I will never leave you.

It's what he told Mira when he made his final decision.

I turn to look at him, but he's just standing there, smiling. "It seems we have the day to ourselves."

———

It hits me then.

If the loss of Oasis has pushed me right up to the edge of

what I can bear in a year of stacked griefs, the strange vacuum left in Connor's and Kieran's absence and this sad, empty, foreboding stillness is what finally tips the bucket of my tears over.

If Brendan were not here, I'd go into the hay storage area, sit down in the silence with my back against the old wooden wall, and howl like my dogs do when I leave the house. It's primal. My heart yearns for the release. But I don't do that, and instead the tears are just leaking over the trembling dam that has held back a summer of accumulated anguish.

Brendan doesn't say anything for a moment, just letting me have mine. If he touches me, I'll fall apart.

"A cup of tea, perhaps?" he offers, with a little smile.

I jerk out a nod—I don't trust myself to speak, and we head into the house. My knee is hurting—damn the useless thing, damn this wretched body that has taken so much, damn this summer, damn everything. I feel so old. At sixty-two, I *am* old. Irrelevant. Unable even to write another book so that I can give poor Perry his story.

The best days of my life are behind me.

There's nothing ahead but more loss.

The magic of the electric teakettle still brings him joy, and I leave him to it. I retreat to my temporary bedroom and flop down on the bed, face-down, burying my head deep in the sheets so he won't hear my muffled sobs.

When I come up for air—full of snot and tears and red, swollen eyes—he's there, sitting on the couch beneath the icon of St. Brendan.

The tea is on the rug, waiting for me next to my bed.

I hadn't even heard him come in, lost as I was in my misery.

He sits quietly, Brendan the dog pressed against his leg as he drinks his tea, and the truth comes pouring out of me like a confession. The guilt that I couldn't save my mother. That I didn't do more. That I didn't see through the illusions she created to protect her independence, her agency, her dignity. That I couldn't be with her at the hospital after her fall to advocate for her, protect her, fight for her—because if I'd done those things, maybe she'd still be here.

I failed her as a daughter.

I failed her because I fell for the illusions. I didn't push harder. Didn't force help. Didn't override her refusals, her furious insistence: *I'm not having anyone wipe my ass.*

I failed her because she died alone.

I reach for the consolation I've clung to since the morning Chris called from her house. If there is an afterlife, she is no longer suffering. No longer trapped in a failing body. If there is an afterlife, she is free, now.

No longer old.

Young again.

It's thin comfort.

If I had loved better—stayed more vigilant, overridden resistance, not trusted illusions—then maybe she would not have died the way she did. Maybe Maisie wouldn't have either. Because I'd failed Maisie, too, putting her through chemo because I wanted more time.

Because I wasn't ready to let go.

Outside, the wind moves the shrubs beyond my window. The windchimes sound unsettled. Urgent.

It's a long time before Brendan speaks.

"You didn't fail her," he says softly. "You honored who your mother was—even when it cost you."

I nod, jerkily.

"Your mother chose how she would live—and how she would not. To take those choices from her, to force her into situations she resisted, even out of love, would have been to take her life away from her before it was finished. To take her dignity. Love is about witness, not coercion. Because denying someone their choices? That, my friend, is a theft." His voice softens. "And you loved her too much to do that."

I put my face in my hands and resist the urge to rock back and forth as his words land in places that had gone numb over the past months, and in that moment I recognize the cost of loving deeply—too deeply—in a world where I don't get the final say—and shouldn't. It is not something most people can hear. It is not something friends who disappear can hold.

He is right.

When does love become witness—and when does it become theft?

And for the first time, I understand that wanting to save someone and wanting them to stay with me are not the same thing—and that love may mean trusting what the author has already written—and knowing when to let go.

When to let go.

My mother defended her authorship by refusing help.

Maisie endured treatment because I wasn't ready to release her.

And Brendan—

I don't finish the thought.

I only know that time feels narrowed. Borrowed. As though something essential has been waiting for this moment.

He rises, takes the empty mug, and leaves me sitting in the quiet as he moves back toward the kitchen.

His words remain.

They settle.

You didn't fail her.

You honored who she was—even when it cost you.

27

I find him standing at the kitchen sink.

The house feels strangely empty. Even the dogs are silent. I hear the windchimes on the front porch singing, clanging, making their own random song. The ones out in the back yard, too, a keepsake that we brought home from Bar Harbor many years ago, deeper-voiced, heavier, a haunting *gong... gong...*

Brendan is looking out over the back yard. There's a Bradford pear that my parents planted many years ago shading the patio, and he's watching the wind turn its shiny green leaves inside out, upside down, showing their silvery undersides instead. Whenever I see upside-down-leaves, I think of my sailing instructor, Steve, telling me a dozen years ago that when I see them, it's a good indication *not* to go sailing.

"Faith, it's a good day for a sail," Brendan says.

What?

He turns and looks at me.

"We should go soon. The wind won't wait."

I don't want to go. I'm scared.

Too much wind.

But I sense that if I don't go, whatever he has come here to show me, to teach me, will be lost.

I *have* to go.

I know that.

And he knows it, too.

I put the dogs out one last time. Find my bag, my water shoes, and the SUV keys. I'm wearing my T-shirt from Denver, a place I know I will never visit again. Brendan's back in the blue Newburyport shirt he was wearing at the dentist's. He's found Connor's forgotten Red Sox cap and it sits neatly over his greying hair, giving him a boyish charm that belies his sixty-five years of lived experience—most of which I've witnessed.

I say most of which, because I didn't stay with him at the end, and it haunts me.

And the drowning, the unthinkable suffering...it is still coming for him when he goes home.

A day ago, I was trying to outrun what had already been written.

Now I know that I have to let him go.

Mom.

Maisie.

Your expectations of what life is supposed to look like.

Let him go.

We get outside. The wind is bending the grasses, whispering through the stand of pine trees on the hill. My boat sits where it's been for the past year, forgotten—surrendered to arthritis, injury, depression.

I get into the Pathfinder, back out into the street, reverse again into the driveway using the SUV's backup camera to line up the trailer hitch, rusty with disuse, against the matching coupler of the trailer itself. It's a mating that must be done just right; I'm not strong enough to push five hundred pounds of boat and trailer across the grass to line them up perfectly. There...there... *there*.

Close enough.

I get out, leaving the door open because usually this is a two- or three-attempt pass, and I need to see how close I've gotten and then try again. I've missed the mark by about six inches. Brendan has never seen a boat trailer up close, but he's already leaning down, grasping the long aluminum tongue, and hauling it toward the hitch so I don't have to get back into the truck for another attempt. Innately, he knows how the hitch and the coupler work. Where they go, how they're supposed to fit. Probably a guy thing. I crank the jack back down, *clicketty-clicketty-clicketty*, and the tongue lowers, the coupler kissing the ball of the hitch and dropping neatly down into place with a satisfying *thump*.

Brendan is standing back, watching me with a little smile.

Letting me do this.

And something—just a little something—is waking up inside me as I look at the sad, rusty ball of the hitch sitting neatly where it was meant to be all along.

We strip off the tarp that's covered the boat since last winter. Beneath it sits the fitted covering, tied down with my clumsy knots that this seasoned mariner must think are painfully inefficient, amateur. He doesn't say anything, of course. The wind, impatient, grabs the covering as we peel it back, tugging it from my hands as if it wants to help. From the now-bared cockpit, the scent of a year's worth of sunbaked fiberglass and wood and flotation devices wafts up, the aroma of summers lost, reminding me of the freedom and carelessness of better times.

Of youth.

Brendan has moved around to her stern, admiring the skiff's heart-shaped transom, her lovely lines, the elegant dash of teak coaming, the functional oars tucked up underneath the gunwales that, as the gusting wind catches my ponytailed hair, I know we're not going to need. He's not only a sailor, he's also a naval architect—and he recognizes a fine, fine craft when he sees one.

I use the strap ratchets to snug the boat down to the trailer. I lock the coupler into place, tuck the jack away, cross-hitch the tie with the safety chains, plug the trailer's electrics into the SUV's bumper receptacle. The electrics still work despite a year of disuse, and my foot on the brake pedal fires the trailer's lights and blinkers.

We're ready to go.

And then Brendan is moving up along her beam. He stops next to her bow, and there, he reaches out to run his fingers over the name I gave her when I bought her to celebrate my fiftieth birthday—a long time ago, when life was still good.

When age and chronic pain and loss and fear had not yet diminished me.

Kestrel II.

Once, there was the real thing.

She deserved to be remembered.

"Ahh," he says, the little crinkles at the corners of his eyes only adding to his smile, and he gets into the passenger seat beside me.

The branches of the fruit trees overhead are all jumping up and down in the wind, rustling with movement, and I feel a stab of fear. At least on the lake I usually sail on, it'll be somewhat sheltered in this wind.

Safe.

I take a deep, steadying breath, my stomach a bit fluttery, and turn to my companion.

"Are we ready to go to Lake Attitash?" I ask, shifting down into drive and feeling the sudden lurch of the trailer and its precious cargo leaving the rut it had sunk into over a year of stagnancy.

Of being forgotten.

"Attitash?" His face shifts to amused disbelief, the mischievous sparkle in his eyes making him look like the man I first met when I wrote him as a young, eager, ambitious Royal Navy flag captain all those years ago. "Oh, no, my dear. We're not going to a quiet little lake."

I stare at him in dawning horror.

"We're going to find salt water." And then, holding my gaze: "Newburyport."

28

The wind is out of the west, just as last night's meteorologist had predicted—hard and clean, the kind that makes halyards clang against aluminum masts, pennants stretch sharp toward the Atlantic, whitecaps leap and break into flying spray.

We're back at the American Yacht Club. The usual group of old sailors sits in the wicker rocking chairs that overlook the waterfront. I've spent hours among them—listening, writing, eating takeout—and hearing their sharp judgments of people who go out on days like this and end up on the *Morons of the Merrimack* Facebook page.

I wonder if I'm about to end up on that page myself.

They're not out in their boats. Nobody is. Maybe the wind is too much for them today, too. In any case, a few of them are watching as I unstrap the skiff, clip a painter to her bow, and wrestle with the wooden mast. I usually step it easily at the lake, standing on the beach. With the boat still on the trailer, I'm too short to manage it.

Brendan takes the mast without comment. For him, height isn't a problem. The mast slides cleanly into place and sits happily in its little cup deep in the bow, catboat-style. I fit the sprit and snotter, then the boom, slot the rudder with its attached tiller into its stern mount, and make sure the mainsheet will run free.

Brendan stands back, approving.

And I can see that all of the old guys shooting the shit over on the long deck are now watching us. A few more have come out from the building itself and have gathered at a picnic table, pretending indifference. The wind is steadier here than it was back home, stronger, and I can feel a dozen eyes on me as I climb back into the Pathfinder and ease the Melonseed down the slick ramp toward the water. Brendan walks the dock beside her, holding the painter steady, keeping us straight. I feel more than hear the satisfying sigh as the water swallows the trailer wheels and the boat lifts, freed at last. I step out, the cold seawater swirling around my calves, release the winch, and push little *Kestrel* out into the flood.

My hair is whipping from my ponytail. It's flattening my shirt against my back, trying to slam my boat into the dock.

Oh God. What am I doing?

Brendan tethers her securely to the dock cleats while I park the trailer. The tide is coming in hard now, slapping against the shore with force.

My heart is pounding. I'm sharply aware of the eyes on us.

I know these men. And because they know me—my caution, my fear of risk—I can almost hear them.

This oughtta be interesting.

Too much wind for her.

Someone's laughing.

And that poor old dude with her...wrong day to take a friend out for a ride. Hope he can swim.

Little *Kestrel* bobs impatiently. Her single wooden mast scrapes the sky with the push of wind and water. Out in the river, the westerly fights the incoming tide, shoving the water into whitecaps.

We pull on our PFDs. I'm not sure I can get down into the boat with my weak knee. I'm pretty sure that I don't *want* to. Brendan lifts me easily and sets me down amidships, and I lower myself to the teak grating; there are no seats. The boat rocks beneath me. Already untying her, Brendan steps down into the stern with the nimble ease of a far younger man as I lower the centerboard. He takes the tiller, pushes the boom over to catch the wind, and the boat shoots out into the river like she's been flung from a cannon. The water is screaming past the bows, and I'm shaking.

Nauseous.

I want to go back.

I can't do this.

He sees it immediately—my clenched fists, the panic in my eyes, the same look I had coming back from Denver last year, when heavy turbulence nearly broke me. With an easy motion, he brings the skiff about and she instantly exhales, startled by the sudden check. The tanbark sail luffs in protest. The wind comes dead over the bows now, leaving her helplessly in irons. We rock up and down, held now by tide instead of sail.

I feel ashamed. Of my fear. Of myself.

Brendan sits quietly, hand resting on the tiller, looking at me with infinite patience.

"Would you like me to bring you back?" he asks, gently.

I can barely speak.

"I'm scared," I whisper.

He nods and says nothing, his body moving easily with the swells as they pass beneath us.

"And they're watching," I add, mortified.

"I know," he says. "Ignore them."

The wind tugs at his borrowed cap. He pulls it down and waits...quietly.

This is the moment.

I know it is.

"Will it be safe?" I ask in a little voice. "We won't capsize? Nothing will break?"

He meets my eyes.

"I can't promise that."

The words land clean and honest. No reassurance. No rescue. Only truth.

Time stretches. The wind tugs at the sail and whistles past the mast. The boat rocks beneath us. I cast a longing glance back toward the dock.

And then he speaks again.

"Tell me," he says gently, "why you chose the Navigator as your patron saint."

I swallow. "Because...he came to me a long time ago?"

He waits, one brow slightly lifted.

It's not the right answer, and we both know it.

"Because he trusted what he could not see," I add, my voice firmer now. "Because he set out into the unknown with no promise he'd ever come home safely. Because he believed life still had more to offer—even when he was old."

He smiles, his eyes warming.

"You're close."

"I chose him because he gathered up his faith, trusted his author, and made the leap out into the unknown—"

"That's it."

And with that, he pushes the boom out of irons.

The sail fills with a thunderclap.

The wind locks in, hard and clean, and the boat heels sharply—so sharply that my breath catches and my hands fly out to catch the gunwales. Cold seawater slashes over my fists, soaks my clothing, and for a dizzying moment I wonder if we'll capsize.

I needn't have worried.

Brendan is already there, weight shifted, the rudder responding to his touch. The sheet runs clean and fast through his hand before I even understand what the wind has asked of us.

I hold on, tight.

Nothing about him is hurried.

His movements are small. Exact. Final. As though the next moment has already arrived and he is simply acknowledging it, a choreographed dance between himself and the little boat.

The skiff surges forward, freeboard deeply awash now,

spray flying up and over the coaming, salt lashing my cheeks. Another gust slams down the river and he eases without looking, lets the sail breathe just enough—out, out, then a touch back in—so the power stays clean and the hull drives hard beneath us.

He doesn't fight her as I might've done.

He *converses* with her.

We are not careful.

We are not safe.

We are moving.

The river is standing up now—westerly hard against the tide, whitecaps breaking sharp and fast—and little *Kestrel* answers him like she's been waiting for him all along. She lifts. She runs. She tacks, jibes, heels, and flies, slicing the cold incoming seawater with a confidence I have never felt at the tiller myself.

I risk a glance back toward the Club.

The men in the wicker chairs are no longer rocking.

One has leaned forward, elbows on knees. Another has stood. A third has lifted binoculars, not bothering to pretend anymore.

No one is laughing.

No one is talking.

Just silence.

And I understand, with a sudden, dizzy clarity, that this is not luck, or nerve, or showing off in heavy wind.

This is the captain I wrote about.

A man who learned his craft in an age when this skill was survival, not recreation. When mistakes were fatal. A Royal

Navy-trained master who reads sea, sky, wind, and current the way other men read letters.

For him, this wind isn't reckless.

It isn't frightening.

It's merely *there*.

Brendan never looks back at our audience.

And if he even sees them, he doesn't care.

He sits on the gunwale, cap pulled low against the wind, tiller alive but steady in his hand, and the little Melonseed runs beneath us like a racehorse finally loosed. He lets her gallop for a while, then hauls in the mainsheet as he brings her about; she answers him with sweet obedience, settling close-hauled now on the port tack, her shoulder buried deep in the water, her bow wake racing past the fingers I trail over the side.

Another gust slams down the river, and Brendan answers it intuitively. Sheets of saltwater pour over the coaming and surge back over the side. My feet are awash in it. My lips taste of it. A watery arc rises up behind the rudder, foaming in our wake, a classic rooster-tail. The hull slams and lifts and slams again, and I am soaked through, laughing now, breathless, terrified, and exhilarated all at once.

He looks at me and grins.

I grin back.

This is better than the concert I gave away.

Better than the music.

Better than anything I could have imagined from the safety of land.

And it's better because I did not stay behind.

I did not stay on the dock and watch.
I'd learned when to let go.
I stepped out.

176

29

———

We drive to Plum Island as the sun hangs low and molten, the heat finally loosening its grip on the day. The sand is glowing pink and orange. The air is filled with salt and the wind that terrified me hours ago has spent itself entirely, as if it gave everything it had, and now wants only rest.

The parking lot is nearly empty—a gift for a woman with a convalescing leg.

"They must be at the concert by now," I say, wishing I could see Kieran's and Connor's joy in what I had given them. And when I think of them there, singing along with eighty-thousand people and dazzled by lights and sound, pounding energy and a sheer abandonment they'll never know in their time, I feel a profound and perfect peace.

All is right in the world.

For now.

I push away thoughts of what they—and this man beside me—will be going back to, refusing to let anything intrude on this perfect moment.

Refusing to consider that he is in the last days of his life.

Don't think of that. Any of it.

You've made the choice to let him go to meet his fate—now honor it.

177

Honor him.

We move slowly down to the beach, my knee hurting (I don't care anymore, let it hurt), my body humming with that deep, earned exhaustion that feels like proof of life. Better than that; proof of life, *lived*. Brendan pulls off his sandals and dangles them from his fingers, enjoying the way the cool sand swallows his feet.

The Atlantic spreads out before us into forever, doing what it has always done.

Wave after wave, uncountable and eternal, folding itself onto the shore with a sound that feels older than language. The same surf in my time. The same in his.

We sit side by side and lean back onto our elbows, faces tipped toward a sky beginning to bruise purple and gold. He looks younger here, unguarded, his cap on backwards the way Connor had boyishly worn it.

I am not afraid now.

The sail has wrung that out of me, and what remains is something quieter. More dangerous.

Inevitable.

I remember his gentle words earlier this day, when I'd poured out my anguish about my mother, and how he'd helped me understand the true cost of relinquishing authorship out of love. Sitting here beside him now, I know we don't have much time left. He will soon return to his own story—and I will let him go.

His story is not mine to interfere with.

Not for what it would cost him.

Not for what it would cost Connor or Kieran, or the

lives that will branch quietly from theirs, waiting in a future I don't get to rearrange.

Oh, God, this is so hard.

But I have to know.

Knowing isn't the same as controlling the outcome, and I've lived with the anguish of what I'd not stayed to see, for far too long.

"So," I say lightly, because I cannot put weight into what I'm about to ask him, "you're a naval architect. You design ships."

"Yes," he agrees easily, closing his eyes for a moment, tipping his head back, and inhaling deeply of what's left of the sea wind.

I trace a groove in the sand with my heel, pretending this is an idle curiosity instead of a question that has haunted me for more than a decade.

"What happens," I ask, carefully, "when a ship of your time, sinks?"

He doesn't turn toward me. He doesn't sense the trap because there is none. It's a door to understanding, and I'm glad I'm sitting down because even now, I know I can't bear to hear it—even as I know I *have* to hear it.

I have to know what he's going back to.

"Well," he says, thoughtful. "It depends."

"On what?"

"On the sea state. The damage, if any. The circumstances. How quickly she takes on water. A good vessel will fight it for a time." There's affection in his voice now, as there always is when he speaks of ships. "Bulkheads and hatches buy you minutes. Sometimes more. Sometimes less."

"And...the people?"

"If they're on deck and lucky, they're swept clear." He shrugs slightly. "If they're below..." A pause. Not ominous. Just factual. "Gravity does the rest."

I stop drawing in the sand. The words land somewhere deep and cold inside me.

"How?" I ask, in a little voice.

He tilts his head, considering. "If you're belowdecks, you could be thrown about. Furniture breaks loose. Anything unsecured becomes dangerous. The ship can roll, sharply, at the end. Violently." He shrugs. "It's not dramatic, really. More...sudden."

Sudden.

He lifts the cap and rubs his forehead, the salt crusted at his temple. He looks out over the sea. The breeze—what little remains of it—stirs his hair.

Just enough.

The greying curls at his temple lift and for a fraction of a second, the dying light strikes something it had not touched before—

And I see it.

Not blood. Not gore. Nothing grotesque.

Just the quiet, unmistakable truth of bone meeting force.

A healed wound, pale and faint. A thumb-shaped mark where there should have been a gentle curve—the smooth line of bone subtly wrong, flattened where it should have risen.

My blood runs cold.

And in that moment, I understand.

The wound is unsurvivable.

My breath leaves me in a single, soundless rush and my head swims with vertigo.

"Oh," I whisper—not because I mean to speak, but because my body cannot hold the word inside.

He turns then, puzzled by the sound.

"What is it?"

I don't answer.

Because in that moment, I realize there's nothing to halt, nothing to prevent. He is not returning to an unfolding timeline the way his sons are. There is no longer any need to torment myself over what awaits him, to suffer the anguish of what I have been dreading.

Because what I have been dreading has already happened.

And the lie I've carried for twelve years—the images of terror, the thrashing panic of seawater filling his lungs, all the horrors my mind invented because I lacked the courage to witness his final moments—collapses under the weight of something far kinder.

I didn't stay to watch.

Not because he didn't matter—but because he *mattered too much*.

The knot in my chest breaks open, and I see clearly, at last.

Brendan did not drown.

He was not afraid.

And he was not alone.

Kestrel—the other great love of his life—had not let him suffer. She had delivered swift mercy. She had taken care of her captain just as she always had, and held him to the end.

The surf keeps coming.

The sun keeps sinking.

And I understand, then, that truth does not always look like rescue.

Sometimes it looks like *release*.

<h1 style="text-align:center">30</h1>

———

We are quiet on the ride home.

It's dark now. The nights are getting shorter in late August, and you can feel it—zippered hoodies as the evenings cool, the leaves looking tired, the maples just beginning to hint at the color that will set them ablaze in a few more weeks. The night air carries a chill that wasn't there a week ago.

The sense of time coming to an end.

My phone has been blowing up all the way back from Plum Island. I don't answer it, of course. Eyes on the road and all that.

Brendan, his face glowing in the occasional passing streetlight, looks tired in a way I have not witnessed since he arrived.

After what I'd seen on the beach, I don't know what to make of it.

I don't know what to make of anything anymore, really.

Maybe trying to make sense of things that don't make sense is the way we get ourselves into trouble. In its own way, it's just another way to control things.

And so I just drive, the tires humming beneath us, the

183

constant ding of my phone as someone plies me with text after text breaking the silence.

We're home at last. I back the boat onto the lawn, and unhitch her. I'll spray her down tomorrow, remove the unfamiliar salt water. The stars are out. The night feels chilly after the warmth of the day, and the crickets are shrilling the way they always do this time of year—high, desperate, almost screaming their protest of summer's coming end. I've always found it haunting—a desperate cry to hold onto life against the inevitable coming of the dead season.

They are especially loud, tonight.

I slap at mosquitoes as we head to the house. Chris has made supper for us; he's like that. Kind, caring, and a good cook. It's his special macaroni and cheese, hot out of the oven.

At last, I pull out my phone and, as expected, there are dozens of texts from Connor and a few from Kieran.

"This is INSANE. I'm hoarse with the singing! They opened with *F'ckin In The Bushes*, and I could feel the bass reverberating in my chest and oh, the SOUND of eighty-thousand people erupting in a cheer as they came out! I'm screaming. We're all screaming. Kieran as well!"

Five minutes later:

"The lights! The sound! The entire STADIUM is singing—this is the BEST night of my life!"

One from Kieran:

"Thank you for this; it was the most wonderful gift that you could've given us."

I scroll through the endless texts. Connor's are full of

dyslexic typos, and I take the liberty here of correcting them. They wouldn't make a whole lot of sense unless you know him, as I do. More texts are arriving. Pictures of the crowd, the Gallagher brothers coming out on the stage, Liam with his maracas and holding Noel's hand high, the giant screens behind them. Doesn't appear to be any urine flying, but it's early yet. A selfie of Connor and Kieran, both touting Oasis merch—Connor in a T-shirt, Kieran in a grey hoodie, and Kieran's actually wearing the kind of smile that will absolutely blind Rosalie when she sees it for the first time.

Kieran, joyous.

Precious Kieran.

Precious Connor.

"They're having so much fun," I say softly, and I want to wrap them both up in my heart and keep them there forever.

Peace.

The night goes on. I do the dishes and make tea. Brendan, yawning, lets me take over without his customary eagerness to command the electric kettle. Chris gets ready for bed, early. He's going to have to get up in the wee hours of the morning to pick Connor and Kieran up down in Boston, and I text Connor to see what time the train will get him back.

It's Kieran who answers. "Don't worry about us. We'll find our own way home."

At the time, it doesn't register what he's actually saying. It won't mean anything until the next morning, when he's not there and I realize he's not coming back. None of them are. But for now, the phone is still *dinging, dinging, dinging* as they share their excitement with the person who made it possible for them, and I grin like a fool. I'm enjoying the concert far more through them than if I'd been there myself. Some short video clips. Later, a FaceTime call of sheer noise —excited faces filling my screen, both of them singing into the phone as *Don't Look Back In Anger* soars in its anthemic joy through the speakers.

Brendan quietly goes off into the other room, and part of me wonders if maybe what I'd seen earlier had been a trick of the light.

The phone dings again.

Connor. Backstage selfie with Liam Gallagher, arms around each other's shoulders, both of them full of swagger and hard, raw masculinity.

"I talked a security guard into letting us go backstage. Liam's funny. Says I'm a bloke cut from the same cloth as he is. Actually, he uses obscenities in a way I've never seen them employed, but I'll not include them here."

I smile. Only Connor.

Only Connor.

"Oh, and Liam says hi, and to tell you he'll see you in 2026."

I grin at that.

31

———

Macaroni and cheese. Warm, creamy, homemade. It's hot out of the oven, and the cheesy topping is crunchy after the broiler's kiss.

Comfort food.

Brendan eats little. Given what I'd seen on the beach, I wonder how he can eat at all. How his body can be warm and strong and alive, how he can even be real. And I sense a gathering-inward of his energy, the way people do before a journey that will take everything out of them.

With polite apologies, he excuses himself, declining tea, and walks quietly off into the living room that serves as my current bedroom. Brendan the dog follows him. Chris and I sit at the old eighteenth-century breadboard table, drinking our tea.

I don't tell my husband what I'd seen.

It feels too private. Too sacred to share with anyone, even the man I love most in this world.

We talk for a while, and play gin rummy. Bradford lies under the table at my feet, much the way his mother Maisie used to do.

Maisie.

The grief had been suppressed all summer, and with

Mom dying suddenly only eight days later, Maisie never had her chance to be properly mourned. Guilt assails me.

Chris beats me in the first two hands, and I put my cards down and quietly tell him I'm going to go check on our houseguest.

I stop short in the doorway. My breath catches in my throat.

And there he is.

Not the man who sailed with me today, but younger Brendan—as he was in my dream.

He is half-sitting up on the couch but asleep, deeply so, as if he'd meant to just close his eyes for a moment and lost the battle to stay awake. His head is tipped to the side. Brendan the dog lies trustingly against him, cradled by his right arm. The dog's head is on his chest, one foreleg resting possessively over his thigh. The captain's fingers rest loosely atop the old dog's ribs, rising and falling with his breath.

Above them, the icon of the saint for which they were both named stands guard over the sleeping pair.

A blessing.

A benediction.

A companion for great journeys into the unknown.

My heart fills. The scene is sacred in a way I can't understand, and I know I'm witnessing a completion—something I can't name or comprehend. I stand there for a moment, resisting the urge to wake him. The hair near his temple has parted, obeying gravity, and for a brief moment my hand lifts, tempted to verify by touch that same deeply impossible place beneath the rich and youthful chestnut curls.

It was not a trick of the light.

I stop.

Pull my hand back.

Because to cross that boundary would be a trespass. He has come to show me what I needed to see and teach me what I needed to know. There's no reason to touch the place where he died, for any of that to be less true.

I look away, and down at my dog, sleeping in his loose embrace, and for the briefest heartbeat of time, I see additional legs and a shimmer of something that comes and goes so fast that I'm not sure it was actually even there.

Maisie.

I blink and whatever it was I saw, is gone.

Brendan is still there on the couch, exactly as before—head tipped, hand slack against my dog's ribs, breath slow and even.

Only now he is older again, just as he was when he walked into this room an hour or so before.

Leaving man and dog to their rest under the gaze of the watchful saint, I step quietly out of the room and return to my card game.

———

AT SOME POINT during the rest of the evening—I don't know when—the messages from Kieran and Connor stop coming.

The phone goes quiet in my hand.

No more videos. No more breathless updates.

Just silence.

I know in my heart what it means. They have stepped back into their own journeys. And when I see them again, it'll be as a silent companion, following along with my notepad—watching them, loving them—seeing their lives play out exactly as they were meant to all along because I had made the hard choice not to pull rank as their author.

The choice to let their father make his own decision.

To let him go.

Chris heads up to shower; I put Tilley and Bradford out for the last time of the night. Brendan the dog is at the gate, wakened by the nightly ritual. He barks, once, wanting his turn. More dog swapping, and I let my old boy out into the darkness.

Chris comes back down in his bathrobe to get Bradford, who sleeps with him. We embrace and kiss each other good-night. I hear him and Brendan murmuring a few words in the living room where I sleep before he heads upstairs, and I wait at the door for my dog to finish his business.

The crickets and night insects are loud tonight. Notably so. Their shrilling has reached a pitch of urgency that pulls at my soul as they cry out against the coming end of the season. Sorrow, resolve, acceptance, and an impenetrable emptiness weigh heavily on me.

And I know, suddenly, that I am not alone.

I turn, and there he is.

Brendan.

He is young again, full of life, vital, handsome, richly *alive*—the same breathtaking man who commanded the eyes and hearts of those women in the Newburyport boutique, the same man who had surely turned the powdered heads of elegant noblewomen as a dashing Royal Navy flag captain—the same man who won Mira's heart when he arrived at her home that fateful day in 1778, fished out of the sea by her brother Matthew, the soaked plans for the ship that would become *Kestrel* in his coat pocket.

Mira.

She is waiting for him now; I sense that, and I silently thank her for letting him come to me in my summer of grief.

Of need.

He's still wearing that same Newburyport shirt; a souvenir, perhaps, because he's got his eighteenth-century waistcoat opened loosely over it. His tousled chestnut hair is tied back in its queue, catching an electric bulb's light it was never meant to know, the richness of color, of youth, glowing within each haplessly curling lock. In this moment, he is a man caught between two centuries, already transitioning, and I sense that he cannot be touched.

Cannot be held.

Cannot be contained.

Not that I would contain him; I've learned what he came here to teach, when it comes to containment, control, and refusing to let go.

"I brought you a little something to remember me by," he says quietly, and he is smiling. It's a warm and knowing look, and I notice then that he's holding a large picture. I can see the brown paper backing. The dark edge of a frame.

And then he turns it around so I can see the face of it and holds it out to me.

He's still wearing that little smile, and overwhelmed, I touch my fingers to my lips, trying to contain my emotion. My breath has stopped. I can't speak.

It is a painting, and I know in my heart that he made it himself.

Three Brendans.

The young Saint Brendan of Clonfert, the Navigator, his hair as deep an Irish red as the man standing before me. The Saint is looking down at a boat he holds tenderly in his hands. It's not the curragh he's usually portrayed with, but an eighteenth-century topsail schooner with familiar lines. And beneath those hands is the third Brendan, portrayed as the sleeping newborn puppy he once was. A dog who had been born into my hands.

The Saint.

The man, implied in the schooner.

The dog.

My eyes fill and the image blurs behind my tears; he's still holding it, waiting for me to take it, and I'm afraid that if I do, this will all end.

I know it will.

My hands are shaking as I reach toward it.

"You even had it framed," I whisper.

"The colors...I wanted them to match the green in your upstairs bedroom."

I reach out and take the gift and hold it close to my chest. The edges of the frame are hard and solid and real.

They ground me as they press against my heart. I turn to look out at the patio, waiting for my old dog to come in from the darkness.

Here he comes now, happy, all set for the night.

I turn back to my houseguest.

Where he'd been, there is only the wooden floor, the rug, and space.

He is gone.

EPILOGUE
195

The summer ended, fall came, and in the waning hours of a dreary November day, I sat in the gathering darkness of my mother's still, empty living room with a candle, my prayers, and a jar of holy water.

I had spent most of the preceding months auctioning off her antiques, going through her memories, the things she left behind in this world that could not follow her. Things she wanted me to see, things she would have been mortified had she known that I had. Little things that could no longer lie about how much she had hidden from me in her last weeks and months.

I held that knowledge close, protecting what dignity I could.

Now, with the tiny flame wavering before me, I sat in the gloom and said my goodbyes. The house had been sold. The closing was hours away. I would never stand in this room again. I would not see this house again. It had outlived its usefulness to anyone in this day and age; nobody cares about gunstock corners and wide-board floors and period wainscotting. The house was tired. The buyer would be bringing in a bulldozer.

I had to let go.

It was time.

I had survived watching her purple Dodge Neon being driven off by a stranger. I had survived the pain of sorting her belongings into donations, keeps, and trash. I had survived a painful conflict with a family member, the listing of the house for sale, the lawyer and real estate agent and paying off of the last of her bills and the endless cleaning of two-hundred-year-old floors after every open house. The little slippers and the last of her clothing, which she'd piled next to her bed, had been bagged up. I'd put them out of sight. They still carry her scent. Someday, maybe, I'll have the courage to open the bags up and revisit her, through touch and scent and memories. But not now. Not yet. Maybe not ever.

For now, they are simply held.

Over the coming weeks and months, my leg healed, just as my orthopedist had said it would. Once in a while the meniscus reminds me that it's in there and sometimes I'll need Advil. Dr. Z says I'll need knee replacements at some point. The idea is frightening. Giving up control and putting yourself in the hands of others has always been impossible for me, and anesthesia terrifies me. But someday, I guess, I'll get that TKR, stepping forward in faith for that particular journey with the same trust and relinquishment that Brendan had shown me, back at the dentist's office so many months before.

I hope I will, at least.

The end of 2025, the worst year of my long life with its stacked grief and relentless losses, was a blessing, and as the calendar turned to the clean new days of 2026, I felt the long darkness inside of me beginning to lift. My writing, long dormant under burnout, grief, and depression, stirs faintly within me, like the first signs of summer as I look out my window on this beautiful May morning. I hear the sparrows out on the patio, chattering, preparing for their babies. The lilacs are out, some of the roses, the grass is green and fresh, the leaves on the trees almost virginal in their minty greenery. It's a day when you want to throw open every window in the house to let in the air, the day, the very world—and with abandon, I begin to do just that.

Chris has finished my bedroom. I've moved out of the living room on the floor below and that old room upstairs where I spent my childhood is my sanctuary now, painted and decorated exactly as I want it. Probably good to open them up there as well, I think, and why not take the dust-rag with me while I'm at it?

After all, spring is made for cleaning.

The morning sun is shining through the windows, lighting up the walls, finding the rich mahogany tones in the antique sleigh bed that had been my parents', and then my mother's. It is mine now. It is happy to be mine now, I think; Mom doesn't need it anymore.

The light is perfect in the room, and I shove the old double-sashed windows open to let in the warm, earth-scented breeze.

I turn, and as I always do, stop for a moment at my altar: an 1860s wooden chest that an ancestor had made—treasured by my mother and still holding her most precious things. On top of it rests a candle, my rosary beads, and the centerpiece of it all:

The picture that *he* had given me on his departure.

It sits there in quiet peace on my mother's old trunk, glowing a bit against the Sherwood Green walls, a perfect pairing of color—just as he'd said it would be. It's a reminder of a miracle that seems far away now, but still close enough in my heart to touch and take out whenever I need it.

My three Brendans.

With me, always.

I gently move the dust cloth over the frame, wondering if it still bears his fingerprints, then pick it up. My smile is soft as I gaze down into it, and as I sit there staring at the loving gentleness of the Saint's face, I feel a slight irregularity in the cardboard backing.

I turn it over, and my eyes confirm what my fingers have found.

There is something hidden there.

I sit down on the bed, carefully slide the little clips aside, and the cardboard sheeting falls away. And there it is, a letter, written on ordinary ruled notebook paper, with an ordinary blue ballpoint pen, markers that ground it in our time, even if the formal and almost poetic style of the writing itself belongs to another, far earlier one:

> *My dear,*
>
> *If you are reading this, then I have succeeded in one last bit of mischief.*

I knew you would look behind the frame. You have always been far too curious—and far too brave—to leave a thing unexplored for long. I hope you will forgive me for that small certainty.

You have wondered for a long time whether you failed me.
You did not.

You have wondered whether turning away in that last moment was abandonment.
It was not.

Some things are not meant to be witnessed. You were right not to stay. I did not need you to see my ending. I needed you to live beyond it.

And finally, you wondered whether to trust what you saw on the beach that last day.
You can.

You have carried a burden for many years, imagining suffering where there was none. So let me set this down gently, once and for all.
There was no fear.
There was no pain.
There was no struggle.

One moment I was exactly where I belonged.
The next, I was elsewhere.

If you ever think again of that small iron woodstove

Mira and I enjoyed in Kestrel's cabin — the one with its honest heat and sharp corner—do not trouble yourself. It was not an enemy. It was simply where the world met me. Swiftly. Kindly. Without spectacle.

Kestrel did what she had always done for me. She held me. She was steady and sure, right to the end. She brought me home—not to safety, but to stillness.

There are worse ways to leave this world than in the place that shaped you, with your arms around the one you loved most.

You gave me more life than most men are ever granted. You carried me into years I did not have, across seas I would never sail, into mornings and moments I could never have imagined. You gave me children, and the chance for their lives to unfold beyond my own.

That was not theft.
That was love.

You felt the urge to reach forward and change what was coming. But you did not mistake that impulse for permission. You let us make our choices without reaching in at all. And in allowing me to make my final decision —in not rewriting my ending—you gave me the greatest gift of all.

You do not need me to stand between you and the unknown.
You know how to sail now.

You always did.

The wind will frighten you again. Let it. Fear is not the enemy. Stillness is.

Go where the water is moving.
Go where the light surprises you.

And when you think of me—and you will—do not think of endings.

Think of motion.
Think of the day you chose salt water.

I was never lost.
I was only finished.

With all my affection, and not a single regret,
— Brendan

I sit there for a moment staring at the wall in front of me, where the full-length portrait I'd made of the man himself, caught in his older years in an 1813 peacoat, looks down at me from the lantern-lit gloom of a ship's cabin, his knuckles resting against a desk, quiet, warm, alive.

He is smiling in the portrait.

I tuck his letter back behind the frame where he had left it, seal it up, and carefully set the picture back down on my mother's wooden trunk. And he is right. If I had pulled authorly rank to ease my own pain by writing an escape from the sinking ship, I would have denied him his choice to stay with the woman—women, if you count *Kestrel*—he loved. I would have denied Connor his growth, and tempered the fire that made him who he was. I would have denied gentle, soulful Kieran his beloved Rosalie, whose hands on that fateful day would have closed around an empty line, hauling nothing up from the sea. And I would have denied Liam Doherty, his loyal best friend, the love he waited a lifetime to find.

All those lives and loves, which would have been profoundly altered had I interfered.

I had not been entrusted with changing the story.

Only with telling it truthfully—and then stepping aside.

Because authorship is witness, not control. Because love does not give us the right to reorder the lives of others. Because saving people is sometimes what can destroy them—whether it's your mother, your dog, or a book character you've lived with for the past thirty years.

I get up and go to the west-facing window where in the distance, faintly visible a quarter mile away, I see the silver glint of the Merrimack. There's a cardinal in the pine tree, fliting about, singing. The wind comes up then, and stirs a corner of the blue winter tarp that still covers my little boat, sitting down there in the yard below me.

Waiting for me.

There is a time for grief.

And there's a time to set it down.

I reach into my closet and pull out my water shoes.

It's a fine day for a sail.

ALSO BY DANELLE HARMON

Introducing

The bestselling, award-winning, critically acclaimed

DE MONTFORTE SERIES

"The bluest of blood, the boldest of hearts

The de Montfortes will take your breath away."

 # 1 Kindle Store bestseller: The Wild One

The de Montforte Series

The Wild One (Book 1)

The Beloved One (Book 2)

The Defiant One (Book 3)

The Wicked One (Book 4)

The Wayward One (Book 5)

The Homecoming (Book 6)

The Fox & the Angel (Book 7)

My First Noel (Book 8)

OFFICERS AND GENTLEMEN

Captain Of My Heart (Book 1)

My Lady Pirate (Book 2)

Wicked At Heart (Book 3)

Lord Of The Sea (Book 4)

Heir To The Sea (Book 5)

Never Too Late For Love (Book 6)

Also:

Heart of the Sea Wolfe

The Admiral's Heart

When to Let Go: A Memoir of Grief and Witness

Featuring bleoved Characters from Officers and Gentleman

THE NOBLE LORDS

Master Of My Dreams (Book 1)

Taken By Storm (Book 2)

My Saving Grace (Book 3)

Scandal At Christmas (Book 4)

STANDALONES

Pirate in My Arms

ABOUT THE AUTHOR

New York Times and *USA Today* bestselling author Danelle Harmon has written twenty-two critically acclaimed and award-winning books, with many being published all over the world and translated into numerous languages. She and her family make their home in New England with numerous animals including three dogs, an Egyptian Arabian horse, and a flock of pet chickens. Danelle enjoys reading, photography, spending time with family, friends and her German Shorthaired Pointers, and sailing her Melonseed skiff, *Kestrel II*. She welcomes email from her readers and can be reached at Danelle@danelleharmon.com or through any of the means listed below:

A small press bound by the belief that every voice matters.

Sign up for our newsletter to learn about new releases and more.
https://oliver-heberbooks.com/subscribe/

Follow us on social media:

facebook.com/oliverheberbooks

instagram.com/oliverheberbooks

amazon.com/oliverheberbooks

youtube.com/@OliverHeberBooksPublisher

www.ingramcontent.com/pod-product-compliance
Lightning Source LLC
Chambersburg PA
CBHW031025160726
47991CB00005B/1874

9798900431307